Halloween

TALES OF TERROR

OTHER LIVING DEAD PRESS BOOKS

OTHER BOOKS IN THIS SERIES

THE ZOMBIE IN THE BASEMENT
CHILDREN OF THE VOID AND DARK DREAMS
THE JUNKYARD
THE HAUNTED THEATRE

OTHER BOOKS OF HORROR

DEAD HOUSE: A ZOMBIE GHOST STORY
CHRISTMAS IS DEAD: A ZOMBIE ANTHOLOGY
BOOK OF THE DEAD: A ZOMBIE ANTHOLOGY
BOOK OF THE DEAD 2: NOT DEAD YET
THE LAZARUS CULTURE: A ZOMBIE NOVEL
THE WAR AGAINST THEM: A ZOMBIE NOVEL
END OF DAYS: AN APOCALYPTIC ANTHOLOGY VOL. 1-4
DEAD WORLDS: UNDEAD STORIES VOLUMES 1-7
REVOLUTION OF THE DEAD
KINGDOM OF THE DEAD
THE MONSTER UNDER THE BED
DEAD TALES: SHORT STORIES TO DIE FOR
ROAD KILL: A ZOMBIE TALE
DEADFREEZE AND DEADFALL
SOUL EATER AND DARK PLACES
BLOOD RAGE AND DEAD RAGE
THE DARK AND DEAD THINGS
RISE OF THE DEAD
VISIONS OF THE DEAD

THE DEADWATER SERIES

DEADWATER
DEADWATER: Expanded Edition
DEADRAIN
DEADCITY
DEADWAVE
DEAD HARVEST
DEAD UNION
DEAD VALLEY
DEAD TOWN
DEAD SALVATION

HALLOWEEN TALES OF TERROR
Copyright © 2010 by Living Dead Press

TALES OF TERROR

EDITED BY
ANTHONY GIANGREGORIO

TABLE OF CONTENTS

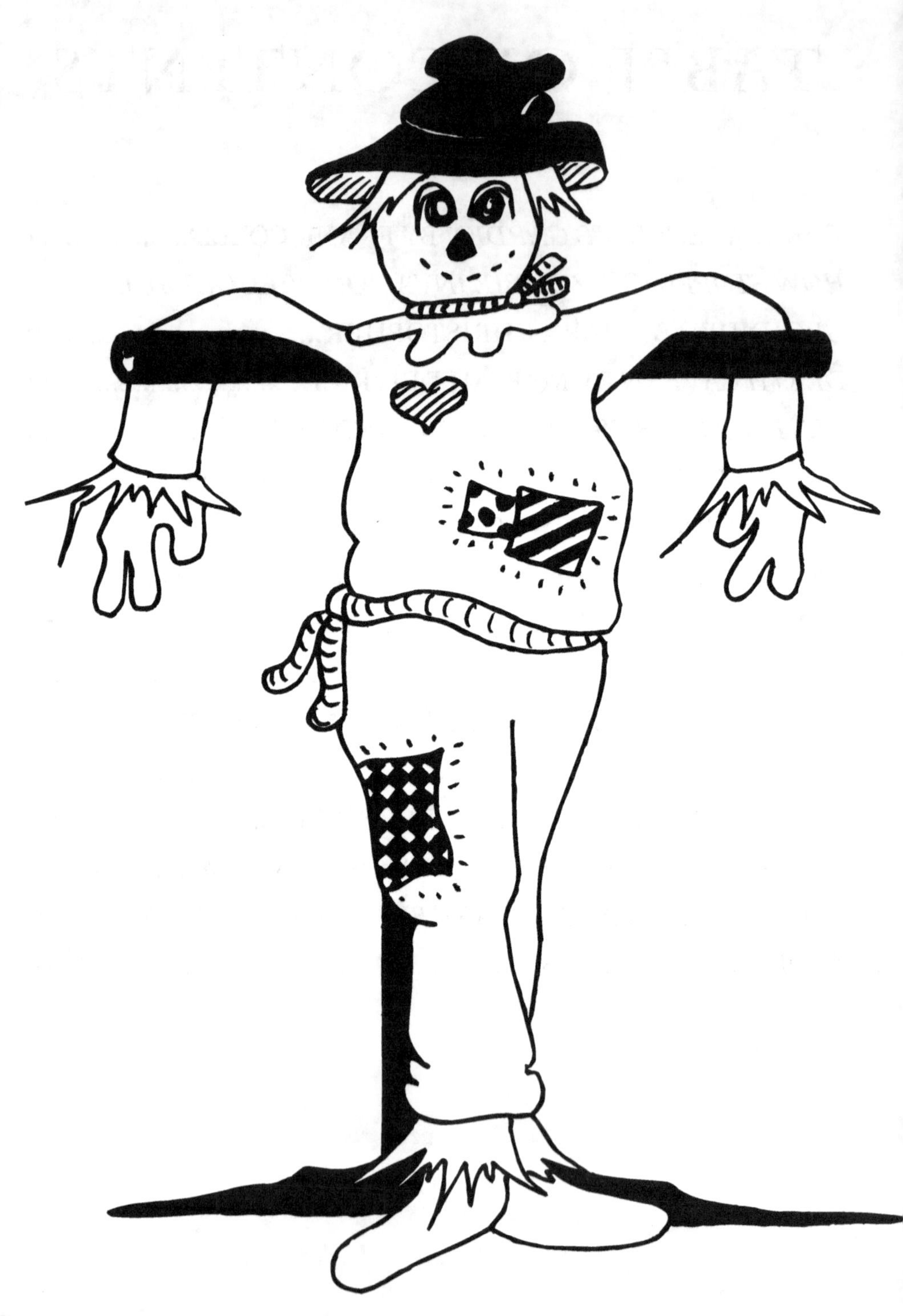

THE SCARECROW'S GARDEN

FRANK COLLIA

Dusk broke the afternoon, light caving in under the weight of darkness. The day's refreshing autumn breeze gave way to fall chill. It was that cozy niche between shorts and parkas the locals called 'sweater weather'.

Brendan Simms called it cold. He no more considered himself a local than he did a kid. He was eleven after all.

It was never like this back in Phoenix where the temperature rarely dipped below warm, even during the deepest stretch of winter. But here they were, in Pennsylvania of all places, a state he knew only from maps and geographical spelling quizzes. Who, he wondered, would ever accept a job in such an uncharted part of the world? He knew the answer was his father, but he still had no idea why.

If any good came out of the move, it was that now he could wear his favorite Arizona Cardinals sweatshirt more than two days a year. It was red with white lettering, memorializing the team's shocking conference championship and, despite its age, looked as fresh as the day it came off the rack. Brendan knew this was very little consolation, but he also understood that, for the time being, it was all he had.

"A fair. I don't know any better medicine for cheering someone up," his father said when the first advertisement appeared in the paper weeks ago. "And what better way to spend Halloween."

"I don't know," Brendan said. "Trick-or-treating with my friends would be better. Back home."

"But a fair," his father said, as if repeating it would make his point clearer. "On Halloween. You can dress up."

"I don't want to dress up," Brendan said. "Plus, we have fairs back home. Better ones."

"First, this is your home. And, how do you know they're better?"

"I just know."

"Actually," his mother said, "I think they're calling this a carnival."

"Listen, it doesn't matter what it's called," his father said. "There'll be rides and...and funnel cake. Who doesn't like funnel cake?"

"I don't," Brendan said.

"Don't give me that. You once ate so much that you missed school the next day because your stomach still hurt."

"Our finest moment as parents," his mother said.

"Fine," Brendan said.

"Fine," his father smiled. "We're all going to have a good time whether we want to or not."

Bundled up and brimming with the anticipation of now proving his father wrong, Brendan followed his parents down the path of crisp fallen leaves to the reveling encampment on the far side of the church's picnic grounds. He tried not to look up, tried to avoid succumbing to the lights, swirling and flashing and pulsating with fun. He tried, but one glance was hook enough, and hooked he was.

The music was what did him in. He trudged along, head down, his ears slowly attuned to the ages-old dancing cornet and organ notes beckoning to one and all. However, there was something off, something different only detectable by inattention. To Brendan, the tone was not as playful as usual, less an invitation than a call akin to his mother's dinnertime shouts.

Curiosity raised his head and he was helpless to look away. By the time they reached the entrance at the mouth of the makeshift wooden fence, Brendan knew his cause was lost.

A weathered gothic wagon greeted them as they approached. It was dust-covered and in disrepair, appearing as if abandoned on that very spot centuries ago. Along the side was scripted ***Malsanto's Rolling Carnival***, the words seemingly formed in the wood itself.

All Brendan could see from his place in line were tent tops, no games or rides, not even the colorful arc of a Ferris wheel. He was surprised, but relieved he wouldn't have to endure another telling of his parents' first kiss.

"That's something," his father said, fumbling for money in his wallet. "I thought it was a law that they had to have a Ferris wheel at these things."

His mother laughed. "Brendan, did we ever tell you about the time we got stuck at the top..."

Brendan knew they couldn't possibly have expected him to care as much as they did about the story and wished they would stop pretending otherwise. He shut them out and focused on the exotic smells intoxicating the night air. He was no longer cold, and hungrier than he had thought possible.

"Didn't these things used to be cheaper?" his father asked as they stepped past the ticket booth.

"We're here to have fun, remember?" His mother patted Brendan on the head.

His father sighed. "Well, let's go see how much fun they're charging for a beer. C'mon."

Brendan didn't move. He wasn't sure that he could. The view from outside had served no justice to the scene before him. Row upon row of neon-lit gaming booths and junk food vendors chained his imagination, sights and sounds and scents that paralyzed him with wonder and delight. Bulging bluish-gray tents, the tops of which had impressed him little, now enraptured him as Mecca's of mystery. Immediately to his left, dazzling a crowd of younger children with sleight of hand, a barker, wildly garbed as a...

"Brendan."

His father retraced his steps back to his son. "We'll see everything. Let's just get something to drink first. How about a shake?"

Delaying visceral gratification was the last thing on Brendan's mind. He shook his head. He wasn't going anywhere.

His father began walking away, but stopped when he realized he was alone. The carnie trickster had transfixed his audience, Brendan in their ranks, with nothing more than a series of dime store coin palms and an even cheaper looking costume. Clichés, however, were meaningless to children and it would take more than ice cream to break the spell.

"Wait here," his father said. "We'll be right back. Okay?"

Brendan nodded and edged closer to the group. Absent-minded recognition turned his head and he raised his eyebrows in acknowledgement.

"Okay. Stay here," his father said and then became part of the crowd as a momentary jolt of freedom left loneliness in its wake. The cold set in and Brendan shivered as he turned back to the gathering. No one was there. People were everywhere, laughing and eating, hustling off to this amusement and that attraction, but no one was where they had been, no one he was expecting to see. He turned around again, a full circle, eyes darting frantically for traction, nothing, and then he saw him, exactly where he wasn't a second before.

There was silence as the festive throng faded into background irrelevance. Brendan hugged himself for warmth. Finally, he said the most obvious thing that came to mind.

"Are you the Cat in the Hat?"

"I'm *a* cat in a hat."

And, so he was. Beneath a tall black top hat, the long man's sideburns had grown thick and bushy, framing his face. Fiberoptic whiskers sprang out of inflated cheeks and the tip of his nose had a dab of dark paint that glistened as if still wet. He wore white gloves and an old-fashioned tuxedo with a curling furry tail poking out from under its tails.

"What's your name?" the cat asked.

"Brendan."

"That certainly is a name." He removed a pad and pencil from an interior pocket, jotted something, and quickly returned them out of sight. He did a two-step jig, ending with hands on his hips and an undeniably feline grin.

"Welcome to Malsanto's Rolling Carnival...what was it again?"

"Brendan."

"That's right. The hallowest of eves to you and yours, young Brendan."

When Brendan only responded with a slack-jawed expression, the cat continued, "Though your lack of ceremonial attire does nothing to warm my festive heart."

"Huh?"

"Where's your costume, boy?"

"I didn't wear one."

"You're a live one, are you? Too old for some holiday cheer? Too cool, too chill, too chili pepper, as the kids say."

"Kids say that?"

"Say what?"

"Too 'chili pepper'," Brendan said.

The cat clapped his paws. "Oh, you kids and your slang."

Brendan looked over his shoulder, his parents lost to the masses. He turned back and forced a smile of too many teeth.

"Well?" the cat said.

"Well," Brendan repeated. It was nearly a whisper.

"Well, let's get onto it, shall we?"

He spun on his heels and popped a baton out of somewhere on his person. Waving the two-foot black wand overhead, he motioned Brendan to follow.

"Where...where are we going?" Brendan asked, nervously looking every which way.

"A marvelous question," the cat replied, "but one, I'm afraid, you should have asked before you started going."

Brendan stopped. They were at the back flap of the nearest tent, a structure seemingly growing by the moment. He felt ridiculously small.

"Now, now," the cat said. "We really haven't much time."

"My father told me to stay..." He pointed to where he thought he had been, a plot of turf now indistinguishable from any other. He moved his finger to the left, then up, then back to the right. He knew he had to have been some place.

"Your father told you to stay? Not to move?"

"Yes."

"Yet you moved."

"Yes."

"Right. What's the problem then?" He tossed the baton from hand to hand, his eyes steady on the boy.

Brendan had seen those eyes before. It was in a novelty catalog his friend Marcos—back in Arizona where he actually had friends—had brought into school. There was an ad for gag contacts, different colors and designs like Jolly Rogers and eight balls—and cat eyes. However, something told him that the eyes gazing upon him now had not come by mail.

The cat removed his hat, flipped it twice, and placed it back atop his head. "You were watching me when your father left, correct?"

Brendan shifted from foot to foot and nodded.

"Ergo, he has implicitly consented to you watching me."

"Um..."

"Ergo, where you watch is as irrelevant to our circumstances as the watch you wear. You do know what 'ergo' means?"

Brendan shook his head. He felt goosebumps infecting his skin.

"Secret to a friend," the cat said, teetering over on one leg, hand cupping his mouth. "Neither do I. I heard it once from a man on a horse. Come." He hopped back onto both feet and disappeared into the tent.

Brendan edged toward the opening. Again, he looked back, sure he wasn't more than a few yards away. The crowd near the ticket booth was thinner now and it was obvious neither of his parents had returned to claim him. He figured he had a few minutes and he *was* curious. And it would make for a good email to Marcos. He slipped inside the tent.

A handful of hanging lanterns barely lit the space. There was a narrow corridor of boxes and crates that ran out of sight along the curve of the tent. It smelled bad with a hint of awful, like one of the countless farms surrounding his new town, and Brendan looked down to make sure he wasn't standing in anything he would regret later.

"Magical, isn't it?" The voice from behind made him jump. He turned to see the cat balancing the baton on the tip of his index finger. "Don't worry. It gets better."

"Maybe I should wait for my parents."

"You could," the cat said, "but I doubt they'd have anything more interesting to show you."

"I meant..."

"From tongue to ear, mine to yours, we'll be back in two shakes of a lamb's tale. Fair?"

A shorn and wobbly ewe shuffled out of the shadows, sniffed the cuffs of Brendan's jeans, and continued on its way.

"Ah," the cat said. "You are familiar with figures of speech, are you not?"

He did not wait for a response, but marched past Brendan in the direction the sheep had come. Brendan bit his lower lip and followed around the bend.

The passageway sharply doubled back halfway around the tent. The odor grew more pungent the deeper they went and it didn't surprise Brendan in the least when he stumbled over a chicken. The bird cackled at his inconsideration, but didn't press the matter.

"Where are we?" Brendan asked.

"So, it's finally asked." The cat wheeled around beneath a lantern, his exotic features alternately mesmerizing and frightening in the dancing light.

"Who are you?" Brendan asked.

The cat playfully bopped him on the head with his baton. "Well, which shall it be? Person or place?"

"Are you Malsanto?" Brendan was feeling more at ease, time providing security, justifiably or not.

"Do I look like Malsanto?" He bent over, his top hat blocking the lantern. The sudden darkness erased any thought Brendan had of comfort.

"I don't know what Malsanto looks like," Brendan said, backing up a step. He thought he heard the whine of a goat nearby, and stopped.

"You know what I look like," the cat said. "Don't you?"

"Yes, but..."

"But, but, goose." The cat straightened and slid to the side. The rediscovered light crashed onto Brendan's face in a brighter wave than he remembered. Shading his eyes, he glanced to his left only to see a rather large goose beneath the cat's off-putting grin. "Next question."

Brendan was aware his mouth had opened and even more aware that nothing was coming out. He wanted no more than to be standing back outside, waiting for his father to bring him a milkshake. The thought of the cold drink sent his body shaking.

"Where..." the cat said.

"Where...are we?"

"Why, we're here." He tossed the goose aside and ushered his guest through a smaller, curtained opening.

Before him, Brendan saw the barnyard scene he had been imagining. Some more chickens pecked here and there, a sow lumped beside a trough, and two goats stood doing nothing much at all. The scene continued beyond them, but the poor lighting masked further revelation. In the near distance, to his right, Brendan saw wooden posts in the grass with a limp rope hung between them.

"Is this an...?" He couldn't think of the word. An exhibit? An exhibition? Or a little of both?

Seconds passed before Brendan registered that he had received an answer to a question that never passed his lips, but by then it was too late. The tent went dark. Considering how dim the lanterns had been, its effect was startling. Brendan felt as though nothingness itself had descended upon him.

"Don't be afraid of the darkness," the cat's voice whispered in his ear. "We are alone in the universe, but for darkness."

Brendan stood his ground, not certain how long he could stand the damp, sour breath on his face, but even less certain if he had any choice in the matter.

The lights returned and, again, Brendan had difficulty adjusting to what was a subtle, at best, change of brightness. He looked up at the cat that apparently, was waiting for just such a cue.

"Brilliant," he proclaimed, spreading his arms in praise and marvel. From the corner of his eye, he noticed

Brendan's locked gaze and gently nodded for the boy to look across the tent.

"What?" Brendan asked.

"I said, 'brilliant'." He unleashed his arms again, although a bit less enthusiastically than before.

"No," Brendan said, "what did you say about the darkness? About us being alone? I heard that somewhere before."

"Well," the cat said, lowering his raised paws with a sigh, "and this is only a guess, but I believe you heard it about a minute ago. When I said it."

"No, I mean I..."

The cat hooked his baton under Brendan's chin and turned his head. "I don't have all night, son."

A spotlight shot Brendan in the face as he turned, forcing his eyes closed, fast and tight. The cat cleared his throat and Brendan reopened his eyes, squinting cautiously at first. The light had spun around to reveal the completion of the barnyard milieu. At the far end of the tent, a scarecrow hung above a small patch of dirt accented by symmetrically planted green sprouts. It was a garden, Brendan realized.

"The Scarecrow's Garden," announced the cat, fervor returning to his showmanship.

It was a generic scene, but perhaps that was what was so hypnotic. The sheer ordinariness was an obvious facade—but for what? Brendan combed for clues, but superficially, reflexively. Splayed on a wooden cross, the scarecrow's head sagged on its chest, its face hidden by the angle and an oversized felt hat. It appeared more sad than frightening, as if resigned to an eternity of hanging in watch over a false domain, a cruel, mocking joke.

Brendan waited. This was a show of some sort, a performance carnival-goers paid to watch, and even in Pennsylvania, no one would pay to watch this. Something was going to happen and soon. The cloaked figure now emerging from the remaining rear shadows was a good start.

The scarecrow's cruciform rotated slightly away from the front of the tent as the hunched figure approached. It was impossible to distinguish size, shape, or features beneath the heavy, black garment, but Brendan believed it to be holding, cupping, something in its hands.

The cat, now atop a short barrel, addressed a non-present crowd of spectators. "Behold the ancient powers of fear! The debilitating consequences of fate! The ungodly terror of...the Scarecrow!"

He crouched down beside Brendan and said, "We're thinking of adding music for this part. For the drama of it all, of course." Brendan didn't respond. What could he say?

The cat rose and lifted his baton high overhead. "Release the..."

His mouth had barely opened when the man, the person, the thing, in the cloak, who Brendan decided was not crouched, but short, no taller than himself, threw up his hands, releasing a plump, black crow. The bird took flight as if emerging from the very fabric of the cloak. Its wings expanded, flapped twice for balance, and it squawked in celebration of its return to the air.

And then it dropped to the ground, dead and heavy as a stone. Brendan glanced up and saw the scarecrow's head return to its flaccid state.

It had moved.

"Did...did..." Brendan stammered and pointed.

"Yes, yes, he did." The cat hopped down from the barrel and yelled, "What was that?"

This time the cloaked figure did drop to a knee, its head lowered, grazing the garden's bed of dirt. Brendan stumbled backward, finally slamming into a wheelbarrow propped up against yet another crate. He regained his footing and braced himself.

The cat continued to bellow. "Haven't we rehearsed this ad nauseum? That's rhetorical, though my current nausea is literal. Stand up. Get on with it."

The figure rose, but looked as if it had no clue what to do next. The cat turned to Brendan and rolled his wild, animal eyes. "It's so hard to find a competent crow wrangler these days," he said as if shooting the breeze at a PTA meeting.

He returned his attention to the source of his frustration. The mysterious assistant motioned behind him, which only succeeded in further raising the cat's ire. "No, no," he said, waving his baton madly. "No more crows. They don't grow on trees, you know." He placed his hand to his mouth, and over his shoulder, said to Brendan, "I know because we've tried." Then, shouting again, "We'll have to do a dry run!"

With a feline grace, the cat returned to his barrel and reassumed his previous position. "Behold," he said, "the ancient powers of yada, etc., yada." He rolled his hand. "Now you go."

The assistant tossed forth his hands, but rather than setting free a bird, he methodically leapt forward, flapping his arms and doing what can only be described as the world's worst impression of a crow in flight. Brendan would have laughed if he hadn't remembered to look up and to the left. When he did, he didn't know if he would ever laugh again.

The scarecrow's head lifted, its body shifting on the cross, wriggling organically. It was not a trick or an illusion. There was no doubt that it was alive.

Everything slowed, became still. Brendan's vision narrowed, focused on the two figures, people, creatures, before him. The one in the cloak seemed to understand the gravity of the moment, like a fawn learning too late the danger of lingering at the stream.

The scarecrow's face was out of Brendan's sight, but the same wasn't true for the prancing assistant. There was a faint, hollow cry and then the sound of his body collapsing.

The cat dropped to the ground and shook his head. "Not again," he said, more agitated than concerned.

Brendan raced for what he prayed was the exit. He lowered his head, not looking at the cat, and certainly not the scarecrow. He hurdled one of the apathetic goats and came down hard, crashing face first into the vegetable bed. A puff of dirt briefly clouded his vision, and when it subsided, he saw he had landed inches from the fallen crow keeper.

Despite everything in his being telling him to get up, to run, he peeked at the body. The hood had lifted back, exposing flesh, identity, raised blue veins on sunken, porcelain skin. The face was that of a boy, not much older than himself, his eyes frozen in inhuman fear.

Brendan's feet scratched for traction, his legs pumped, his kinetic energy pushing him frantically away. He regained his bearings and hit the entry flap of the tent on a dead run, tumbling into the cool fall air, into the moonlit night, into remembered reality.

His foot clipped the wheel of a baby stroller and Brendan once again tumbled to his knees. As the passing reprimand from the stroller's owner sounded distantly, he looked up with half-expected shock from the ground. The front of the tent said nothing of scarecrows or gardens. There were no warnings or disclaimers. There was, however, a large, colored print promoting the world's fattest woman.

"Never before have you been witness to a human female of such incomparable girth," the cat said, strolling out of the tent, his face alive with hucksterism. "Your eyes will expand beyond their physical limitations in order to capture the enormity of what lies in wait. She may appear more animal than person, but I assure you she is as genuine as the girl next door just on a much...much larger scale. The world's fattest woman—some call her Orca, we just call her Meg."

Brendan got to his feet and turned toward nothing in particular, but more importantly, away from something very specific. He would find his parents and everything would be fine, safe, and in a day or two, or maybe even by morning, he would have forgotten whatever it was that he had seen.

"Brendan," the cat said.

The voice pierced his intentions, and despite having no reason to stop, to turn around, he did.

The cat's hat towered above the crowd, the rest of him visible in glimpses between passersby. What was clear was that he was again writing something into his little pad.

"Brendan," he repeated. He raised his head. Their eyes met. "Do tell your friends."

HOW STOPPING A ZOMBIE INVASION WILL GET YOU GROUNDED

MARK CHRISTOPHER

"I call this meeting of the Monster Hunting Club to order," Mark Sino exclaimed as he banged a small hammer on a piece of wood serving as a makeshift table.

Immediately, the buzz of conversation inside the small, tin shed drew to a halt. Mark stood facing the crew of three boys, all sitting like Indians on the concrete floor. He was tall for his age, taller than most eleven year old boys, and his dirty blonde hair sat unkempt atop his head.

Seated in front of him were three of his closest friends and cofounders of the M.H.C.; or the Monster Hunting Club. With the television being dominated by people hunting ghosts, Mark and his friends were intrigued if they could uncover any spooky situations in their small town. Over the past year, they had had some great adventures, but none resulting in a positive creature sighting.

"Ron, will you please read the minutes from last week's meeting?" Mark asked, as a short, dark-skinned boy stood up.

Ron Webbles adjusted his glasses and spoke in a clear voice, reading off the crumpled piece of loose leaf he held in his hand.

"After a thorough investigation, Paul's werebeast turned out to be his neighbor's black cat, Tapioca."

"Dude, I don't care what any of you guys say! That thing is mean and has it out for me!" Paul Gegens said as he leapt to his feet. His olive skin and dark hair were total opposites of Mark, even though the two were first cousins

Ron continued. "Also, Corey's swamp hag was revealed to be his sister with a mud mask on her face and curlers in her hair."

"And I have proof!" Corey Westlie shouted as the chubby boy with curly black hair jumped to his feet and produced a photo.

Mark took one look at the photo which revealed a girl covered in green gunk and a surprised, angry expression on her face. He had to admit, it was indeed the most terrifying evidence they had captured.

"So we have nothing. No monsters as usual," Mark said with a look of disappointment. "Well, do we have any new leads? Maybe a new place to investigate? And where is Nick? He should have been here an hour ago."

As if on cue, Nick Boats crashed into the room.

"Hey, guys, sorry I'm late!" Nick said with a shout.

"Dude, you scared the heck out of me! Not cool!" Paul shouted and the thought made Mark laugh to himself. Nick was short and scrawny with a box hair cut. He was not a picture of intimidation.

"And where have you been?" Mark asked as he eyed the book Nick was cradling under his arm.

"I found this really cool book at the library. I started flipping through it and I just lost track of the time. It's called *The Art of Dark Magic*," he said as he handed the book to Mark, who took one look at the book and immediately got a funny feeling. The book's cover was crude and appeared to be leather. The words were stamped to the front with black ink. There was no author or any other information printed on it.

"I figured maybe we could use it to pull some Halloween pranks. Like maybe do something to Mrs. Maria for giving us apples every year," Nick said with a shudder. He hated apples; especially the non-candied variety.

"Or maybe on Mr. Leo; he always gives us toothbrushes!" Corey said.

"What if we brought a zombie back?" Paul asked as a smile spread across his face. "Just one! That would freak them out!" Corey added.

"Well, let's see what they have in here," Mark said as he flipped through the book. The others watched over his shoulder as he flipped through the thin, weathered pages.

He passed *How to Make Items Levitate, How to See the Future, and How to Disappear.* Halfway through the book he found it. *How to Raise the Dead.*

"Yes!" Ron exclaimed as he pumped a fist in the air. They all began to talk at once, a muddled sound of excited voices. Suddenly, a louder voice brought their meeting to a close.

"Mark! Come in and help us set up for the party!" Mark's mom called from the house.

The Sino's Big Halloween Bash was a party thrown every year and one that was looked forward to with great anticipation. The entire neighborhood turned out for the event. Each year the party grew bigger and wilder, and with Mark being older, it meant he was able to help with the labor of setting up.

"All right, we'll meet up here tomorrow night and head to the graveyard," Mark said.

"What about trick-or-treating?" Paul asked.

"We'll have plenty of time to do that," Mark said. "Let's just see if this actually works. And if anyone wants, you're more than welcome to help me setup for the party."

He was answered by four voices, all offering an excuse to why they couldn't stick around.

"Whatever. Meeting adjourned," Mark said as he brought the hammer down on the plank of wood.

Mark entered his home through the back door off the patio and walked into the kitchen. The kitchen and dining room had been morphed into a playground of fake spider webs, plastic skeletons, and paper ghosts. He didn't see his parents as he rested against one of the counter tops.

Suddenly, a werewolf with a ferocious snarl on its face leapt from behind a wall! Mark screamed and closed his eyes.

"Happy Howl-oween!" the werewolf yelled with a laugh and Mark recognized his dad's voice.

"Ha ha, very funny, Dad," Mark said sarcastically as his mom rounded the corner from where his dad had just launched himself.

She was balancing a metal tray in one hand and had a pumpkin tucked under her arm. She removed the mask from Mark's dad's face with a quick tug.

"Will you stop playing? You still need to arrange the tombstones in the front lawn!"

"Yes, your majesty," he said with a small salute and then a bow. All three started laughing.

"You know Halloween brings out the kid in me," he said as he lightly kissed his wife's cheek before walking to the front yard to construct the graveyard.

"You needed me, Mom?" Mark asked.

"Yes I do, dear. I need you to fill the brain mold with Jell-O. There are twenty molds and they'll be the centerpiece for tomorrow night's buffet. I want to make sure they have plenty of time to set."

"Sure, no problem," Mark said as he eyed the boxes of strawberry Jell-O stacked on the counter like a flimsy tower.

Mark boiled the water and added the packs of gelatin to the liquid. The chemical smell of strawberry-flavored gelatin was pleasant to him; however his mind was miles away, thinking if it was possible to raise the dead.

It was Halloween night, and Mark stepped outside and greeted the cold, night air with a howl. The air was crisp and the sky was cloudless as a full moon hung overhead, casting its light down and making shadows dance and come alive.

He was dressed as his favorite Teenage Mutant Ninja Turtle, Leonardo; equipped with a plastic sword. Paul was with him and was also enjoying the night. He was dressed like a G.I. Joe with a camouflage shirt and pants to go with his plastic gun. His parents had arrived at the party early to help. Mark could already hear 'The Monster Mash' blaring from the speakers inside his house. A mummy and a vampire walked up and Mark recognized Nick and Ron.

Nick had the book tucked under his arms. Corey was last to arrive and was dressed in a red jump suit; he was Super Mario.

"Let the Monster Hunting Club begin!" Mark yelled happily as they walked to the cemetery.

The cemetery wasn't far from where Mark lived, only about four blocks away. Paul pushed open the iron gates and the group walked in. Mark had passed by the cemetery many times during the day and the image never scared him. At night, however, it was very different. The trees were bare of all their leaves and the limbs were twisted and beckoned like the claws of an old hag. The moon cast a pale light down and the headstones appeared to glow. Mark was sure he saw things moving behind the protruding stones.

"I'm scared," Ron said.

"Don't be a baby," Mark told him, not wanting to admit that, he too, was scared.

Most of the graves in the cemetery were old and had fallen into disrepair, weeds growing around the cracked headstones. However, there were some fresher looking graves towards the center of the graveyard. The M.H.C members stood in front of the new tombstones in a tight line.

"Well, here goes nothing," Mark said as he opened the book and began reading from the marked page. "Eeshay Keeshay Komish Nomish! I call up the dead! That is my wish!" he shouted into the silent night.

Only silence answered back.

"This is stupid, and we're missing out on candy!" Paul whined.

Suddenly, an icy wind blasted them; sending goose bumps and chills running though their bodies.

"Did you feel that?" Ron asked as he looked down at his feet.

Before anyone could answer, the ground shook softly. Within seconds, the gentle vibration morphed into a tremendous jolt as the M.H.C members fell to the grass. Mark could see the ground split and separate over the fresher graves. Then there was silence. Only the sound of their breathing could be heard and Mark was sure someone could hear the beating of his heart.

A dull, hollow moan escaped from one of the graves. It was answered by another; and then another. The boys stood up and saw a pair of gray, moldy hands shoot up from the split earth.

Ron and Nick had seen enough and turned to run.

"Wait!" Mark shouted. "Let's see what happens."

From the opening in the ground, a man pulled himself up from his grave, stood up, and slowly shambled towards the group. Mark could see he was dressed in what was once a nice black suit. His hair was stringy and most had fallen off his head, which was little more than a horrific looking skull with sunken eyes. The man's mouth hung in a slacked position and his hands were stiff and resembled claws. As he took a step, worms and other bugs fell from him and scurried to find a new home.

Mark stepped forward and said, "We woke you! You will listen to our commands!"

The zombie looked perplexed for a moment as Mark reached out his hand. Quickly, the puzzled look was gone and in its place was a look of hunger. It fell forward and landed on top of Mark, sending both of them to the soft grass.

"Get it off me!" Mark screamed as he grabbed the zombie's shirt collar, stopping the snapping jaws from making contact with his neck. A foul odor escaped the zombie's mouth as it tried to bring its face closer to its meal.

The others rushed in and grabbed the man by the suit jacket. They dragged him off and sent him tumbling backwards as Mark leapt to his feet. Their victory was only momentary as they realized they were almost completely surrounded by the walking dead. Men, women, and even a few children, all in various stages of decomposition, stared at them with hungry, dead eyes.

"Run!" Corey yelled as the boys sped towards the iron gate and ran out of the cemetery. They made it two blocks before coming to a stop, all bent over as they sucked in as much air as they could.

"Let me see that book," Mark said as he struggled to catch his breath. Nick was holding onto it and handed it over.

Mark flipped to the page with the spell he had just read. He glanced at it quickly and turned to the next page. There was an entirely different spell on the next page. Mark noticed the page between his fingers felt thicker and realized two pages had stuck together.

Using his fingers to separate the pages, Mark read the remainder of the spell. "Warning: Zombies will crave brains immediately after reawakening. They cannot be controlled until after they eat."

"Nick, you dolt!" Mark yelled, "There was more to the spell!"

"Me? You were the one reading it!" Nick argued back.

"Stop it, guys! What are we going to do?" Paul asked with a look of fear.

The gentle night wind carried with it the moans of the dead as they made their way out of the cemetery.

"I got it!" Mark said as an idea popped into his head. "Paul, come with me! The rest of you, distract our undead guests. Get them to follow you back to the cemetery."

"What should we do?" Corey asked, not liking the idea.

"How should I know? Just don't get too close to the zombies and be careful!" Mark shouted as he and Paul ran down the street.

"Where are we going?" Paul asked.

"To get them some brains!"

The two boys arrived at Mark's house and were greeted by a room full of monsters and movie stars.

"Boys!" Mark heard his mom call out from across the room. She was dressed as a police woman. "Come say hello to your grandma."

"There's no time! The zombies are coming!" Mark screamed at her as he ran to the food table. In the center, amongst the finger sandwiches and cheese dip, was a large, metal platter with a pile of red Jell-O brains. He grabbed the platter and watched the brains jiggle like fat slugs. He ran out the back door with Paul quickly on his heels.

"Mark, what are you doing? Get back here now!" Mark's mom cried.

"My, they certainly have a wonderful imagination," Mark's grandma, who was dressed as the tooth fairy, said with a laugh.

"We're here!" Mark yelled as he and Paul entered the cemetery.

The scene was one of chaos as Ron, Corey, and Nick played a game of tag with their undead opponents. Mark counted ten zombies total as the boys weaved in and out of the wormy corpses, lightly touching them to get their attention and then quickly retreating.

"Dinner is served! Come and get it!" Mark yelled as he placed the platter on the ground. The Jell-O brains all twitched and jiggled spastically.

Ron, Corey, and Nick ran towards the iron gates and stood next to Mark and Paul. The M.H.C made their stand behind the brain buffet.

Slowly, the zombies lumbered forward, seeing only the tasty looking boys ahead. Then they noticed the platter on the ground and the squishy, red brains. The man who had first attacked them reached down and plucked one that had fallen into the dirt. He brought it to his mouth, paused for a moment to study it, and then slammed it into his mouth. The boys could hear the noisy, wet chewing as the man's jaws made short work of the soft gelatin. The other zombies joined in and soon all were feasting. When the brains were gone, the zombies stood up straight, as if called to attention by an invisible drill sergeant.

"Did it work?" Paul asked quietly.

"Only one way to find out," Mark said as he cautiously stepped forward. "Zombies!" he called and all of their dead eyes focused on him, causing Mark to almost turn around and run home. He fought the fear and pushed on.

"You've had your fun on this Halloween night, but now it's time for you to return from whence you came. I command you to return to your homes!" Mark yelled with authority.

The zombies began to stagger forward towards the open iron gates.

"Wait! No! Stop!" Mark shouted and the undead mass halted. "I meant return to your graves and rest in peace."

Without a sound, the zombies immediately turned back and walked to their graves. Slowly, they crawled back down into the open earth, never to emerge again.

"Now what?" Nick asked.

"I guess we cover them back up," Mark said with a sigh. *So much for trick-or-treating*, he thought.

It took several hours, but they boys got the job done.

"So how 'bout that?" Mark asked as they walked back to his house. "Our first official monster encounter and I think we did a pretty good job."

No one replied.

As they approached Mark's house; Ron, Nick, and Corey split off and headed home. Mark and Paul stood in the backyard.

"I'm sorry we didn't go trick-or-treating," Mark said.

"Sorry isn't good enough," Paul said as he slugged Mark on the shoulder. "You owe me some candy!" he huffed as he stormed off.

Oh well, Mark thought as he rubbed his arm. *At least nothing else could go wrong.*

"Mark Sino you march up to your room this instant!" his mom's voice cut through the night like a knife. "What has gotten into you? Why would you steal my center-piece? Was this your idea of a Halloween prank? You're just like your father!"

She scolded him all the way up the stairs.

"No T.V., no scary movies, no nothing until I say so!" she yelled from the bottom of the stairs. He closed his bedroom door softly and flopped on his bed. He knew they would be talking about it some more in the morning.

Mark sat up and stared out his window and into the night. Halloween was quickly coming to an end and he had experienced a memorable one this year. As he undressed, slid under the covers, and laid his head down, he realized that real life was nothing like the movies.

In the movies, he would have been hailed a hero for stopping the rising zombie invasion. In real life, however, all it did was get him grounded.

There will be much to discuss at the next meeting, he thought as he closed his eyes and dreamed Halloween away.

DEATH CAVERN

MARIAH DEITRICK

"I can't believe we're here," Brad said, smiling from ear to ear. "Good thing we bought tickets early. Look at the line." He pointed to the ticket booth. The line went on for blocks, and cars were still pulling into the parking lot.

"This is going to be awesome!" Josh said, squeezing Angela's hand.

Angela and Jill weren't as enthused about going to a haunted house as their boyfriends were. They thought it was childish, and said they'd have rather stayed home handing out candy.

Death Cavern had a reputation of being the scariest haunted house around, and since they just turned sixteen, they were finally able to get in. The guys were not missing it for anything.

"It better be worth the fifteen dollars we paid to get in," Brad said.

"It won't be," Jill said, rolling her eyes. She'd been to haunted houses before with her dad, and they all had the same stuff; coffins, men with chain saws, and hands grabbing you in dark rooms. *This was surely going to be the same*, she thought.

"Don't say that," Brad said, scowling at her, the two girls laughing. They couldn't believe the fuss the guys at school were all making about this. It was only a fake haunted house. They weren't allowed to actually harm you, so what was so scary about that?

The line moved up then, and their group was next to get in. Brad and Josh were high-fiving each other and some of the guys in line behind them.

"You're up, guys," a large man in a Jason mask said, as he pushed the door open.

Right away a man with a chainsaw jumped out at them. None of them jumped or made a sound.

"See," Jill said. "Stupid."

"Shhh," Brad hissed, grabbing her hand as they walked through the next door.

When the next door opened, they could hear people screaming from up ahead. "See," Brad said. "Scary."

The door slammed shut behind them, and they heard a click. It was locked. Moans started, coming from all sides. It was dark, but they could all tell there were people around them, and within seconds they were being touched. Both guys jumped, but the girls were perfectly still. They were not impressed.

"This is stupid," Angela said. "Totally not worth the fifteen dollars."

"It'll get better," Josh assured her, and he was hoping that was true. So far, it was pretty stupid.

They pushed their way through the grabbing hands and into the next room. This time it wasn't dark. Coffins lined the walls, but they were all empty.

"What the heck?" Brad said, disappointed. "No one's even working in here." He was clearly upset by this. He went over and started poking around one of the coffins.

Josh went to open the next door but it was locked. "I guess the other group is still in there," he said, and they waited for the click for it to open.

The next room was full of blood splattered all over the walls and floor. A man was laying on a gurney with his insides exposed, and another man was dressed up like a doctor. He stood over him, pretending to work. Jill rolled her eyes again. *They could have at least come up with something unique*, she thought, and moved on.

It wasn't until the next room they walked through that either of the girls had any reaction at all, but it wasn't from fear. The room smelled horrible, like rotten meat. They covered their noses, but it didn't help.

"They really need someone to clean this," Jill complained.

"No, this is how it's supposed to smell," Brad argued. "It's supposed to be like rotten flesh. The next room's going to be awesome. I've heard about it." His eyes lit up with excitement.

The others weren't as convinced, but they went in anyway.

The room was lined with rows of bodies hanging from the ceiling, and it was cold. They all shivered, but they had to admit it was the best room so far. Every person was completely still with different cuts and wounds.

Suddenly, the door flew open behind them, making them jump. The man dressed as a doctor came in carrying the man that was pretending to be operated on. Brad laughed. It was all part of the show, he figured. The doctor hung the man up on a hook, turned around, and left.

Brad and Josh walked over to the guy and poked him. They were sure he was going to jump out to scare the crap out of them, and they were trying to get it started. But the man was still. There was no sign of life.

"They sure have great actors here," Josh said, laughing. "He doesn't even look like he's breathing."

Jill and Angela weren't as impressed as their boyfriends, and they started walking toward the next room.

They just wanted it to be over with, and their boyfriends finally followed.

"How long is this thing anyway?" Angela asked.

"Twenty-five rooms," Brad answered animatedly.

"Great," she muttered under her breath. "Let's hurry up then."

Jill agreed with her and they went as quickly as they could past another man with a chainsaw, another dark room, and another with empty coffins. But the next room was a doctor again. It seemed to be the same one they had passed before, but this time there was a girl lying on the table.

"Wonderful," Jill said. "It's twenty-five rooms of the same boring stuff."

The man dressed as a doctor looked up and smiled at her. She gave him a sarcastic smile back, then pushed them all forward to the next room. It was the same smelly room as before, and after that the same room with the bodies.

"This is not cool," Brad said, finally losing interest and wanting to get out, but there was no end. The rooms kept repeating and repeating, but this time there were people lying in the coffins. "Finally, something new," Brad mused, and when he said that, the lights flickered for a second, and then Brad was *gone.*

"Where'd he go?" Angela asked as the lights came back on. They looked in the coffins but he wasn't there. The last one was empty.

"I told you it would be scary," Josh laughed. "He'll be waiting for us when we get out."

The girls nodded and moved on. The same pattern kept repeating over and over until Jill was alone the last time she came to the coffin room. She was glad it was almost over. They would kidnap her and take her out of this stupid place, she hoped.

"Okay, come get me!" she called, but the lights didn't flicker. From behind, the man in the doctor costume came storming through the door and grabbed her arm instead.

He pulled her along, and she followed with a grin until they came to the body room again. Brad was now hanging from a hook. Jill laughed. Great, they get their customers in on it, she thought.

It wasn't until she reached the room with the gurney, and saw Angela lying on the table, that she realized it wasn't a game. Jill ran over to her, but she wasn't moving.

The man walked over to pick Angela up, then took her out of the room. Jill hurried to get out, but both doors were locked. She could hear a group of patrons on the other side of the door, waiting to come in. Jill beat on the door and yelled for help, but they laughed at her. They thought it was part of the show, like she and her group had.

"Run!" she yelled, but that made them laugh harder.

The doctor was back, and he pushed her on the table. He was trying to tie her down, when the door unlocked and the next group walked in. Jill kicked him and flew up off the table, trying to catch the door before it closed and locked again, but the group pushed her back toward the doctor, thinking it was all part of the show.

Jill let out a cry when the man caught her, but the group continued to laugh at her. One of the guys even pointed and said, "Wow, she should be an actress."

Within minutes, the group was gone, and Jill was alone with the man playing doctor. She was trembling as he pushed her down on the table again, trying to tie her down. Several more groups passed through in the process, but all had the same reaction as the first—they were having a good time, and thought it was well worth the fifteen dollars.

Every time a group came in, Jill hopped up and tried to get to the door, but she wasn't fast enough. The doctor finally stopped trying to hold her down because of the reaction she was getting from the groups that entered. He even laughed when she succeeded in her mission, and escaped.

Jill was heading back into the heart of the haunted house, instead of the way she came in. She ran through the doors as the group stayed behind, enjoying the show. She stopped in the coffin room and rubbed her hands along the walls, searching for an exit. It was empty again, but she knew there had to be away out. That's where all her friends had disappeared.

At the exact moment the group behind her was making their way into the coffin room, Jill slide under a cart holding a coffin and into a hole in the floor. She dropped into a dark tunnel that was barely lit by small candles.

She decided she would go to the left because that should lead her under the entrance, and she was sure there was still a huge crowd waiting to get in. She could slip into it easily and disappear, she hoped, but she had to get out first.

With nowhere to hide, Jill moved quickly through the tunnel, listening for footsteps as she went. All she could hear were the screams above her. She was running, frequently looking behind her when, in the gloom, she ran into someone and let out a scream as arms wrapped around her, holding her tight! Her scream was cut off by a hand placed over her mouth.

"Shhh! Jill, it's me, Josh."

She grabbed on to him and started to cry. She thought she was the only one left.

"Have you found a way out?" she asked, even though she knew if he had, he would have probably been gone already, but she was still hoping.

"No, but there has to be a way," he said. "Follow me." She followed close behind him as Josh led her back the way she had come.

The tunnel ended and two more began. Josh shrugged and turned to the left. There wasn't time to be picky. Someone would come looking for them soon. Every tunnel ended leaving two more options. It was a maze with no end. They felt like they were going in circles again.

Jill stopped walking. "We're never going to get out of here," she sobbed. "There's no way out of here, and we can't get out up there." She pointed to the ceiling, and the haunted house above them.

"Yes, we will get out," Josh told her. "We have to keep going." He grabbed her arm and pulled her along.

At the end of the tunnel there were no more options. Josh felt the walls and the ceiling, looking for a way out, but there was none. It couldn't just end, he thought, but it had. There was nowhere left to go except back to try different directions, but that was going to take forever. They didn't have time to try them all, and most likely there was only one right combination.

Jill could feel her legs getting weak. This was the scariest haunted house she had ever been in, and now she wasn't getting out. She dropped to the ground and started to cry, but Josh pulled her back to her feet.

"Let's keep moving," he insisted, and Jill moved sluggishly behind him until they reached a tunnel that looked like it was lit up at the end. The light gave her hope, and she started moving faster.

As they moved closer to the end, they noticed an exit sign was lighting the way. Jill and Josh ran in the direction it was pointing in, and at the end was a large metal door. They both looked at each other, hoping it wasn't locked.

Josh pushed it and was relieved when it opened with ease. On the other side was the rear parking lot of the haunted house. They both let out a sigh of relief followed by a scream when someone jumped out in front of them.

"Wasn't that the best?" Brad yelled animatedly. "You should have seen the looks on your faces."

Jill smacked him. She didn't think it was funny at all. She really thought they were going to die. "You knew about this?" she asked, still in tears.

"Nope," Brad laughed. "Not until I was pulled from the coffin room," he said, sounding proud. "The man in the doctor costume picked you two to scare because of your comment." He looked at Jill when he said the last part, and she remembered the comment she'd made and the smile he gave her.

"Where's Angela?" Josh asked, worried about his girlfriend.

"She should be coming out any minute," Brad said, still smiling, and he was right. Within five minutes Angela came through the door.

"That was way better than handing out candy all night," Angela said, and they all laughed at the fake blood all over her.

"I still don't think it's funny," Jill said, but she was starting to get over it. She had to admit, it was a pretty freaky haunted house. "So, Angela, was it worth the fifteen dollars?" Jill asked her friend.

"Oh, yeah!" Angela answered with a smile. "The look on your face alone was priceless."

ALL HALLOW'S EVE

DANE T. HATCHELL

It was a cool, dry, autumn day in El Dorado, Arkansas.

But it wasn't just any day, for this day would surrender to Halloween night.

For Kade Christopher, it was the night he looked forward to more than any other night of the year; even more than Christmas Eve.

There was a certain magic that Halloween brought, a feeling of unbound energy as he slipped a mask over his face; becoming a creature of the night, or more deliciously, a creature from a nightmare.

Every year Kade started working on his costume earlier than the year before. At his desk lay a stack of hand-drawn prototypes of how he wanted his costume to look this year.

But all that hard work, mostly the efforts of his mother to make it a reality, was behind him. Tonight, the only burden would be carrying all his candy home without spilling it. Well, that and watching over Keaton, his younger brother.

Keaton was six, just two years his junior. Kade wasn't happy that he would be in charge of his welfare tonight. He pitched a fit when his father told him that he was taking Charlie, his two year old brother, trick-or-treating, and that Kade would be responsible for Keaton. It was all about becoming a man, his dad had said.

Kade wasn't concerned about becoming a man. He wanted to be a kid. If it had been up to him, he would have been an only child. He didn't like it when Keaton held him back from the things he wanted to do, and now it was worse with Charlie coming along. At first, Kade told his mom he was going to be a pirate captain this year and make Keaton dress like an anchor. His mother laughed, but knew he was just lashing out.

This year Kade was going to be a zombie. Not just any zombie, but a Doctor zombie. Complete with glow in the dark scrubs, and a stethoscope from his dad's EMT kit. But what was going to make this costume super special was the fake intestines he was going to be hanging out below his stomach.

He actually came up with the idea himself and his dad helped him with the project. Six feet of clear plastic, one-inch tubing from the hardware store was folded, twisted, and hot glued to make a convincing set of intestines. Of which he would fill with a gruesome concoction later.

The final touch was the special face paint that glowed under black light. He practiced applying it and knew just how to brush it on to give it the eerie look of the undead. He would wear a black light LED necklace to illuminate the special face paint.

"Young man, you know the rules. Stay on the main street and don't go by the Folter's place. Don't eat any candy that's not wrapped. Watch for cars and trucks, and look both ways before crossing the street," his mother said, adjusting the bright green surgical cap on Kade's head.

With his arms crossed, Kade asked, "Do I have to take Keaton? He's a scaredy cat. He's going to slow us down and I won't get half the candy I usually get. Can't he just go with Dad?"

"We've been over this too many times, son. Your father will be pushing Charlie in his stroller, and will go too slow for your little brother. It's time you step in and help him grow up to be a big boy like you." Kade's mother was trying to help Keaton become more independent, and figured that tonight would be a great time for him to gain some confidence and become less clingy to her and her husband.

"Where is that little twit anyway? Is he ready? I don't want him to make us late," Kade said.

As if from nowhere, a crash of tennis shoes against the wood floor sounded in the doorway. "Action Man is here to save the day!" Keaton yelled.

"Look at him, Mom, he's not even dressed right for Halloween," Kade said.

"I am too! I'm Action Man. And I can take on a hundred zombies like you," Keaton yelled defiantly, hands firmly on his hips. His yellow and blue costume was specially designed to reflect light for safety.

"I thought you said he was scared," his mother teased. Kade stood in silence, unwilling to admit he was wrong.

"I'm not scared. I have my Action belt to save the day." Keaton moved his hands from his hips and pointed to his father's tool belt that was shortened to accommodate his small frame. The leather belt had various pockets and clips to store things. Keaton had modified it for his cap gun, plastic boomerang, silly string, marbles, and a flashlight.

"Well, all I have to say is that you better keep up with me or I'm going to let the monsters get you," Kade said.

"Kade!" his mother scolded.

"Enough of that, are you ready to fill your intestines, son?" Dad asked, coming out of the garage and drying his hands on a towel.

"Yeah, let's do it," Kade replied.

A can of corn and a can of green peas had been draining in a colander by the sink. Kade helped his dad shove some corn and peas in the tubing, being careful not to pack it too tight.

Dad opened a few light sticks from its packaging and cracked them, allowing the two chemicals in the stick to mix for the bright glow to appear. He then cut the end off one of the sticks, and poured the liquid into the tubing. The peas and corn now were illuminated in creepy yellow-green light. They added more corn and peas, and more glowing liquid, until the home made intestines were full.

"How disgusting," Mom said as she scrunched her nose in distaste.

"Can we go now? The sun is about to go down," Kade said.

"I guess so. It's better to get an early start anyway," his mother said. "Where's Keaton?"

"I'm coming!" Keaton called from the kitchen. He closed his mother's purse and put a cylinder shaped object into one of the snap pockets on his belt.

The two went to the living room corner and put their shoes on. There were four decorated trick-or-treat bags with reinforced handles waiting for them, one bag for each hand.

Dad tied the plastic intestines around Kade's waist, then gave him a congratulatory swat on the rear.

Mom stood at the front door and blew them a kiss as they ran out the door. "Don't forget the rules!" she hollered, and they waved without looking back.

Brown Heights Park was a four street neighborhood just off the main highway. It was a modest development for middle income families. One of the few amenities was that the streets were extra large with many homes on each one.

The main road leading to the subdivision streets ran parallel to the main highway. Each of the four streets connected to the main road in the front, and to a rear road in the back. One single gravel road jutted off the rear road, leading into thick woods. That road led to the Folter place.

Goblins and ghouls, fairies and teddy bears, emerged from houses and invaded the streets. The glow of jack o' lantern smiles appeared on porches and by the side of the road as darkness hid the normalcy of the day and unleashed the demons into the night.

Kade was pleased that Keaton kept right up with him. It was almost a race to see who could reach the next door first.

"Trick-or-treat!" They both would yell, waiting for the door to open, eying carefully the tasty treats that were dropped in their bags.

A dingy looking ghost with dirty sneakers trotted up next to Kade and his brother as they were between houses. "Hey, Kade, I know where there's caramel apples."

"Carmel apples! Where?" Kade could tell the ghost was his neighbor from the next street, Billy Johnson, just from the sound of his voice.

"The Folter place. Old man Folter was fixing a sink at Jimmy's house and told him to come on Halloween night and get a caramel apple."

Kade frowned, although it was hard to tell when a zombie was frowning, "The Folter place? We can't go there."

"I know, my parents told me to stay away from there, too. But Jimmy said he was going. If he's not afraid to go, then I'm not either. Want to come with me?" Billy asked.

"I better not, I have to watch Keaton, and he might tell on us," Kade said.

Keaton was ignoring the two boys and when they were within a close proximity of the next driveway, he darted for the front door.

"Keaton, wait up!" Kade yelled, leaving Billy on the street, and for him to make his trek alone.

The night grew darker and Kade and Keaton had been down their street, up the next, and down the other. The two were now on the connecting rear street, which were vacant of houses and street lights. They were next to the gravel road leading to the Folter place.

There were no other kids on the rear road but them. The gravel road and the woods surrounding it, was spooky as darkness enveloped everything. All dark and filled with strange sounds and angry dogs barking in the distance, Kade found himself swallowing the knot of fear in his throat.

"Let's hurry to the last street, where they have lights," Keaton said. The two turned to head to the next street over, when a man exited the woods and stood down the road from them.

He was tall and fat and wore overalls. He sported a big hillbilly hat, and a beard that hung to his waist. He stood sideways to them and was eating something that made a crunchy sound.

"Mmmmmm, mmmm. My, my, this is the best tasting caramel apple I've ever had," the man said. He was looking forward, not in the direction of the boys, and was talking out loud to himself.

The two boys walked closer, Kade was about to make a run for it when the man turned and faced them. "Well, howdy there, boys, you guys get a bag full of candy tonight?" the man asked.

Kade and Keaton stopped dead in their tracks, "Uh-huh," Kade answered.

"Mighty fine, mighty fine. Halloween sure is a fun time of the year." The man paused, took another crunching bite from the caramel apple, and smacked his lips loudly.

The two boys stood still, as if waiting for permission to be dismissed.

"Say, did you two get you one of these apples?" the man asked, wiping apple juice off his beard with the back of his hand.

"Nuh-uh," Kade answered, now eying the caramel apple with great interest.

"Well, you're missing out on a treat. The caramel's so soft and fresh, and the granny smith apple's crisp and tart. Let me tell you I never had one finer. No sir, not me."

"What did you have to do to get it?" Kade asked.

"Oh, a nice old woman down the gravel road is giving them to all the kids. She has some Halloween decorations in the front yard of her house. Once you pass the decorations, you get to go into her kitchen and pick out your caramel apple. You might want to hurry though, she might not have many left," the man said.

Kade wanted a caramel apple really bad. All he had was store bought candy in his bag, but nothing as special as a caramel apple. Each time he heard the man take a bite, Kade's mouth watered.

"Is it far down the road?" Kade asked.

"Not far at all. You'll be there in no time. There's some dogs close by, but don't worry about them. They're tied up and won't bother anybody. Well, boys, I wouldn't wait too long if I were you," With a wave, the man turned and left towards the next street over.

Kade looked at his brother, "I want one of those caramel apples."

"But Mom said not to go there; that's the rule," Keaton said.

"That man got an apple, Billy and Jimmy got an apple. All we have to do is run down the road and get one too. Geez, we can be there and back in five minutes," Kade said.

"I don't know," Keaton said.

"You're not scared, are you?" Kade asked.

"I'm not scared! But Mom said..."

"We just won't tell her. It'll be our secret. That's part of growing up; you keep secrets. Now, let's hurry and go so we can finish the last street and get home.

"Race ya!" Keaton yelled and led the way down the dark gravel road, Kade close on his heels.

After about thirty yards down the road, it turned and lined up with the front of the house. There were jack o' lanterns lining the road, all the way to the house. The orange flame from the candles flickered, giving them a look of evil.

The two were startled when the dogs started barking. But they could see that they were chained up to some trees by the side of the house, just like the man said.

A table with some displays was set up in front, leading to the porch. Kade couldn't make out what was on them from where he was. But he was afraid to get too close without permission.

There was a large caldron bubbling and generating wisps of smoke in front of the table. Kade and Keaton inched their way up to it to see what was inside.

As the two peered over the top, the shriek cackling of a witch erupted from behind.

"Heeheehaahaahaa."

The two froze, and Keaton grabbed Kade by his left arm, holding him tightly.

"Hello, boys, glad you could make it to my haunted house," a woman said.

Kade and Keaton slowly turned to see a short, gray-haired old woman wearing a big floppy witch's hat, and a flowered covered house coat. She didn't look scary at all.

"My, look at you two. A zombie doctor come to make a house call, and a superhero come to my rescue," the old woman said.

"Yes, ma'am," the two said in unison.

"I bet you're here to have some Halloween fun and some caramel apples. Am I right?" she asked.

"Yes, ma'am," Kade said.

"Well now, let's get started." She walked past them to the cauldron. She took a large ladle and stirred the torrid brew. "It's a combination of fruit punch and dry ice. Would you like some?"

Kade and Keaton were thirsty; they had made quite a hike with nothing to drink since the start. She poured them each a cupful at their request, handing it to them with a smile.

They each quickly drank the cool concoction. The drink did have a sweet flavor to it, but something was different. It had a metallic sort of taste. Something bumped Kade's lip from the bottom of the cup. He looked into it to see what was in it.

A large eye was looking up from the bottom of the cup as he was looking down at it.

"There's an eye in my cup!" Kade screamed.

"Oh, posh, that's just made of rubber. It's Halloween," she said.

"But it looks so real," Kade said.

"That's what makes it fun, right?" she laughed, snatching the cup from his hand. "Now, come and check out the scary things I have on the table."

The uneasiness Kade had first felt upon meeting the old woman was starting to leave him. This was a set-up just like they had at the school carnival, so he knew just what to expect.

Kade whispered to Keaton, "Don't be scared at any of this. It's all fake. I'll tell you about each one when we get to them."

The old woman led them to the first display on the table. In a large bowl was a collection of skin, fat, unidentified pieces of meat, and what looked like pig intestines. A sign above it had **Guts** written in large block letters.

"It's chicken guts," Kade whispered to his brother.

Next they came to a bowl of ***Eyes floating in a Pool of Blood.***

"That's grapes in tomato juice," Kade said.

"They don't look like grapes," Keaton shot back.

Kade didn't want to admit that Keaton was right, but that's what the school used last year.

Bloody Brain was next for them to examine. The brain was a sickly gray underneath a thin sheen of red, and was smaller than the one at the school.

"That's made of jell-o, with peaches in it. Strawberry jelly is smeared on top," Kade said, and he shook the table. But the brain didn't wiggle like the one at school did.

Last on the table was a bowl full of ***Human Tongues***.

"That's canned peaches and red food coloring," Kade said, thinking that the peaches must have been unusually large.

"Okay, boys, that brings us to the end of my Halloween display. Would you like to come in and get your caramel apples now," the old woman asked.

"Yes, ma'am," Keaton said. Kade was silent, lost in his thoughts of what he'd seen. The two followed the woman past two jack o' lanterns sitting on bar stools by the door, and then into the house.

The kitchen was small and the wooden floor creaked when they walked across it. The old woman led them up to a counter where two caramel apples were on a white plate, looking like they had just won a blue ribbon for the best caramel apples ever!

Kade's eyes widened when she picked them up by the wooden sticks shoved into the bottom of each one. She handed one to Keaton, and as Kade's eyes grew wider, one to him.

Kade's teeth entered the cool skin and the caramel sweetness bathed his watering mouth. With determination, he took the biggest bite his little mouth could manage. The crack of the crispy apple filled the air and a spray of apple juice tickled his nose. It was the most wonderful thing he had ever tasted.

Keaton followed with small little bites, sounding like a nibbling mouse.

"You boys enjoying the apples?" the old woman asked.

Each nodded their head in unison, choosing to chew rather than speak.

"My, it does my heart good to see such young boys enjoying themselves," she said to them with a smile.

Now that Kade finally had a caramel apple in his hand, his eyes wandered to a pan on the counter. He assumed it was more caramel apples. But they weren't shaped like apples, and some didn't resemble an apple at all.

"What are those?" Kade asked, pointing to the pan.

"Those? Oh, those are for my husband. He likes other things dipped in caramel too," she said.

"What things?" Kade asked.

"Let's see, that one on a stick is a pear, that one's a banana, these two are strawberries, and the other two are orange slices," she said, pointing to each item. "They're fresh. I just wrapped them up before you two came up."

"How did you know we were coming up?" Something about this entire situation bothered Kade, he just couldn't put his finger on it.

"I heard the dogs barking, no one can get close to the house without me knowing it," she said.

"Oh," Kade crunched down on more of his apple. Keaton was less inquisitive, giving his full attention to his treat.

Kade looked around the room; it was decorated for Halloween, too. Then something he saw gave him pause, his chewing slowed, and his mind shifted into overdrive.

"What's that?" he asked, pointing to a dingy white ghost costume hanging from the ceiling.

The old woman frowned. "It's a ghost. What does it look like?"

Kade swallowed what was in his mouth. "Why does it have a red stain on the back of its head?"

The old woman's face tensed. "I bumped it against some red paint when I was hanging it up."

Kade's knees started to get weak. That ghost costume looked a lot like Billy's.

The sound of footsteps caused Kade to turn around to see a bald-headed, clean shaven, tall, fat man enter the kitchen. Kade recognized him only by the overalls he wore.

"Oh good, I'm so glad you're here. This one was starting to get curious," the old woman said to the man, as if the two boys weren't in the room.

"Fresh or frozen?" the old man asked.

"Frozen, we've got enough fresh for now," she said.

Kade interrupted her, "I think we better go now. We have to get on home, thanks for the caramel apples. They were the best."

The old woman managed a fake smile. "I'm so glad you two enjoyed yourself. You'll have to come back next year and do it again."

"Yes, ma'am," Kade said.

"Say, boys, how would you like to take a picture with Halloween Santa?" the man asked as he dropped to one knee so he was level with Kade and Keaton.

"Halloween Santa?" Kade asked.

"Yes, only special boys and girls get their picture taken with Halloween Santa. Halloween Rudolph is with him, too," the man said.

"I think we need to go home," Kade insisted. Keaton's eyes were going back and forth between the man and Kade.

"Nonsense, it'll only take a minute," the man said as he put a hand into the small of each of the boys' backs and pushed them forward. The old woman opened a door and the man pushed them in. The old woman followed, closing the door behind her.

A large, walk-in freezer took up an entire wall on the opposite side of the room. Kade spun around and turned to leave, but the old woman was guarding the door, holding a rolling pin menacingly in hand. The man still had control of Keaton, and pushed him in front of the freezer door.

The man turned the bar handle a quarter turn down, and a loud mechanical click sounded. He opened the door.

Inside the freezer, on a chair sat a frozen corpse wearing a Santa outfit. A frozen Doberman Pinscher with deer antlers fastened to its head sat at Santa's feet.

Keaton started crying at the ghastly sight, the cold air and putrid smell made his stomach wretch.

"Go ahead, you two, get in there and I'll take your picture," the man said, smiling.

"Don't do it, Keaton!" Kade screamed.

Keaton hit the floor face down, arms glued tight to his side. Keaton used to do this when he was younger and didn't want to leave a place. He would flatten himself out on the floor and offered no assistance in moving. His dad would pick him up like a piece of wood, stick him under his arm, and carry him out. But Keaton was much bigger now and it wasn't as easy to carry him.

"Come on, kid, get your butt in there," the man said, but Keaton completely ignored him. "You're going in there one way or the other, so I guess it's going to be the other."

The man bent down in front of Keaton to pick him up and the man's backside was now pointed toward Kade. In a last act of desperation, Kade charged the man, pushing him with all his might.

The man tripped over Keaton, then stumbled head first into the freezer. Kade quickly closed the door and pulled the handle up a quarter turn; the mechanical click sounded again, and this time it was locked.

"You little monster! You open that door and let him out right now!" the old woman screamed.

Defiantly, Kade ran at the old woman, trying to push her out of the way. The two struggled. Kade held the hand by the wrist with the rolling pin, and the old woman was pulling at his collar with her free hand.

Keaton stood still, wanting to help, but afraid to move.

Kade fought diligently, but his young, undeveloped muscles were no contest against her. Though old, she was still stronger than him. She managed to force him down to the floor, as she raised the rolling pin overhead to end his resistance once and for all.

Keaton reached into his Action Man homemade utility belt, unsnapped a pocket, and pulled out a cylinder-shaped object, the one he had taken from his mom's purse.

He pulled the cap off, ran at her, and sprayed the old woman directly in the eyes.

She let out a scream and dropped the rolling pin, then began rubbing madly at her burning eyes. The irritating pepper spray fumes filled the air.

Keaton helped Kade up. The two ran from the room and slammed the door behind them.

Kade stopped as they ran past their trick-or-treat bags and picked them up.

On the counter, in the pan, were the special caramel delights the old woman had just made. They were too tempting for him to leave, so he scooped them up and put them in one of his bags.

Kade led the way and burst through the front door, knocking both jack o' lanterns off their stools. They crashed to the porch, the candles still burning.

The two ran home without looking back, going straight there, not caring if there was any time left to trick-or-treat.

Their mom was looking out of the window when they ran up the driveway and she went outside to meet them.

"I was about to send your father out to look for you two. We haven't had a trick-or-treater for over thirty minutes. Where were you?" she asked.

"We...we were on the last street," Kade huffed. "We ran all the way here; we didn't want to be late."

"Well, I hope you got enough candy to make it worth your while. Next year you're going to wear your watch, young man. I don't like to worry like this," his mom said, turning and leading them into the house.

A siren wailed in the distance. Dad left out of the front door, the screen door slamming behind him. "I got a fire call. It's the Folter place. I'll be back as soon as I can." The tires of his truck squealed as he left the driveway.

"Hey, Mom, can we eat some more candy before we go to bed?" Kade asked.

"How can you have room for more candy? I bet you ate two pounds of candy while you were trick-or-treating," she said, frowning.

"Nun-uh, we didn't. We hardly had any," Kade assured her.

"Well, tomorrow *is* Saturday. Fine, it's your stomach after all. But if you throw up, you have to clean it up," she said. "And you better brush your teeth extra good before bed."

"*Yaaaay!*" the two yelled, and began digging through the bags of candy.

Keaton came up with a bag of gummy worms, and started eating one by holding the tail end and nibbling at the head as it hung down.

"Oh, how disgusting," she said as she walked away, leaving the boys to their gluttony.

Kade chose the caramel pear. He had never had a caramel pear before and could hardly wait to try it. He carefully pulled the plastic wrap off the outside as he didn't want the caramel to come off with it.

The caramel skin was just as soft and fresh as the apple he had eaten earlier. He opened his mouth wide and bit down hard, ready for the sweet taste of the pear.

But instead of the firm flesh of a pear, he instead bit into something softer and more leathery. He pulled at it with his teeth and something inside stretched, then tore off. His mom walked back into the room with two glasses of milk for them, and she suddenly let out a scream when she saw the blood seeping from the chunk of aorta Kade held in his mouth, red rivulets dripping down his chin.

The left ventricle was now exposed on the caramel-covered heart, dripping blood down his left hand, and on to the floor.

A HARD LESSON

ANTHONY GIANGREGORIO

"Oh, boy, it's finally time to go trick-or-treating!" James yelled as he galloped up the stairs to put on his Batman costume. He had owned it since September and now, finally, it was time to wear it.

It took him less than two minutes to don the gray and black costume over his clothing, then with his utility belt firmly secured around his waist, including his trusty Swiss Army knife, he ran down the stairs, taking the last three steps in one leap. He flew through the air, his black cape blowing behind him, and landed loudly on the floor.

"James! What did I tell you about jumping down the stairs?" His father yelled from the living room.

"Not to do it," James called back.

"That's right. So get your butt upstairs and walk down those stairs the right way, or you can forget about trick-or-treating this year."

James opened his mouth to protest but quickly closed it. He didn't want to get his father mad at him, not tonight of all nights. He glanced at the clock on the wall to see it was ten minutes to six. Richard and Kyle would be ringing his doorbell any second so they could all head out together. Turning, he crept up the stairs as fast as he could, then slowly, ever so slowly, walked down them.

"Good, see? That wasn't so hard, was it?" his father asked.

"No, Dad."

James turned and walked into the kitchen, where his mom was waiting with her arms crossed over her chest and a big smile on her face.

"Your father caught you again, huh?"

"Yeah, he did," James replied.

"Well, just be glad he's in a good mood and he didn't want to punish you."

"Tell me about it, Mom, it's Halloween night for Pete's sake. I've got stuff to do!"

She looked down at her eleven year old son and shook her head. She handed him a cell phone and a pillow case.

"Here you go, just as ordered. I made sure to reinforce the seam, so it won't break if you fill it with candy," she said, gesturing to the pillowcase. "And you keep that phone on at all times. That's the only reason I'm letting you go out there all alone without an adult present."

"Aw, Mom, I won't be alone, the guys will be with me."

She ruffled his hair. "Maybe so, but if I'm not there with you, then to me you're alone. Just humor me, I'm your mother, it's my job to worry."

The doorbell rang and James ran for the front door. "It's the guys! They're here early!" He threw the door open and laughed when he saw his two best friends, each wearing their Halloween costumes.

Richard was a mummy, wrapped with cut rags from an old sheet. Splashes of black and brown paint were added to the rags to make him look really old. Kyle wore a Dracula outfit, complete with plastic teeth, white face, black cape and a large silver cross on his chest.

"Guys, what's up? You look awesome!" James yelled as he waved to his mom who was standing in the hallway. "Hey, Richard, what's up with the cross?"

Richard shrugged. "Nothin', I just thought it looked cool."

"But vampires don't like crosses," he replied.

"So, I'm a special vampire. Crosses don't hurt me."

"Whatever."

"Remember, no talking to strangers!" his mother called as the door slammed closed.

"What did your mom say?" Kyle asked.

"Nothing," James said, waving the question away. "She said to have a good time."

"So where do we want to go first?" Richard asked. The rags covering his face kept falling into his eyes and he had to push them up. It reminded James of a man wearing a hat that was too large for his head.

"Let's go to Third Street. They always give out the best candy there," Kyle suggested as the three boys walked down the sidewalk.

"Great idea," James said. "Third Street it is."

As they walked down the street, they admired all the other kids out trick-or-treating as well. All wore colorful costumes. They saw little girls in princess attire, three more Batmans, a Frankenstein, a zombie, a Superman and a hobo to name a few. It was a clear night and the temperature was in the high sixties. And with the full moon, it was the perfect Halloween night.

Third Street was four blocks over. It was a large street with houses that were huge, with large, manicured front yards and stone walkways. It took longer to get to each house, but the reward was always worth it. Financially a better neighborhood, the home owners always gave out large candy bars and other assorted goodies.

It was as the three boys were walking that a brown beat-up van pulled along beside them. Behind the steering wheel was a man dressed as a werewolf. He had gone all out with long fangs, coarse hair glued to his face, arms and hands, and even under his shirt collar. The passenger side window was open and the werewolf called out to the three boys.

"Hey, boys, you goin' to the party on Park Street?"

"What party?" Kyle asked, intrigued. He was the wildest of the three boys, always getting into trouble.

"Oh, man," the werewolf said, "you didn't hear about the Halloween party? It's gonna be awesome with prizes, food and so much candy you're stomach will explode by the time you leave."

Richard's eyes lit up. "Oh, wow, that sounds cool! Way better than running from house to house to get candy." He looked at Kyle and James and said, "Come on guys, we gotta go there instead!"

"I don't know," James said, not liking where this was going. "Besides, Park Street is almost a mile from here, that's a long walk."

"Tell you what," the werewolf said. "I'm going there now. Hop in and I'll give you a lift."

"That would be great!" Kyle yelled as he walked to the van's cargo door and slid it open. "Come on, guys, let's go!"

James hesitated. "I don't know, Kyle, this seems funny to me. Maybe we should just go to Third Street."

Richard took a step toward the van as he looked back at James. "What could happen, James? There's three of us and only one of him."

James considered that. There were three of them, not the usual child kidnapping his mom always made him worry about. And he had his cell phone if there was a problem. He looked at the werewolf who smiled with his pointed fangs. *Man, they really looked real,* James thought.

Finally, he said, "I'll go, too." He climbed into the van next to Richard as the door closed behind him.

"Great, glad to have you onboard," the werewolf said. With a howl that made James wonder just how good of an actor the man really was, the van pulled onto the street, leaving the bustling trick-or treaters still ambling about on the sidewalk behind.

A few minutes later, James looked out the small window in the door and realized they weren't going to Park Street. The werewolf driver was going in the wrong direction.

"Uh, guys, I'm getting a bad feeling about this," James said. "We're not going anywhere near Park Street." He reached into his pocket and took out his cell phone, but when he looked at the small screen, it told him he had no reception.

"That won't work in here, boy," the werewolf said. James looked up and saw the werewolf's eyes in the rearview mirror. They were now creased and didn't look at all friendly. He pointed at the roof and walls of the van. "They're shielded."

"Hey, what's going on here?" Richard asked, realizing the werewolf wasn't being as friendly as before. "I thought we were going to a party?"

The werewolf laughed lightly, a low chuckle that seemed to come from deep in his chest. He raised his right hand so all three boys could see, and as each of them watched, talons popped out much like when a cat is scared.

"Oh, you're going to a party, all right, only it isn't the one you thought."

Kyle was the first to say it, though all three boys were thinking the same thing. "Oh my God, he's a real werewolf."

The werewolf nodded. "Sure am. My kind love Halloween. It's one of the few times we can hunt for our prey in plain sight. No one gives it a second thought to see a man in a werewolf costume walking down the street...or driving a van."

"W...what are you gonna do with us?" Richard stammered.

"Oh, let's just say you won't like it much. Hey, have you ever wanted your picture on a milk carton before?" he laughed again, long and loud as he turned the van onto another dark street. James could see through the windshield that they were heading out of town. He knew he needed to act fast to save himself and his friends. After all, he was Batman, it was his duty to be clever, brave and save the day.

Richard looked like he was about to burst into tears, he was so scared, and Kyle didn't look much better. James felt that way, too, but he rallied his courage and pulled his two friends close to him.

"Okay, guys, we need to work together if we're gonna get out of here." He reached into his utility belt and pulled out his trusty Swiss Army knife. He looked at it, but knew it wouldn't be enough. Then, James eyes went right to the silver cross hanging on Kyle's chest.

"Kyle, give me your cross," James told his friend. Kyle did as he was told, pulling it off and handing it to James. Then James looked at Richard, and the rags used for bandages. "Richard," he said, "give me some of those bandages."

Richard nodded, sniffling back a sob as he did so. In the driver's seat, the werewolf was humming a song as he drove onto a dirt road devoid of streetlights.

A minute later, James had all the items he hoped would set them free.

"Okay, you guys get ready, and when I tell you to, run to the back of the van." Both boys nodded.

James crawled up to the back of the werewolf, and as he raised his right hand with the cross in it—the silver cross—the werewolf's eyes went to the rearview mirror and went wide when he saw James.

"Why you little..." the werewolf began, but no sooner did he speak then James jumped forward and stabbed the werewolf in the shoulder with the silver cross. The cross was like acid to the werewolf and the beast howled as James pushed the cross in as far as he could. But no sooner did he do this then he used two of the rags to wrap around the werewolf's closest arm. As fast as he could, he pulled back and tied the rags to the back of the driver's seat. Having to drive, the werewolf couldn't untie his arm and he fought to control the van as it swerved across the road.

"Okay, follow me!" James yelled as he crawled to the back of the van. When he tried to open the door, it was locked because there was no handle, but he used the housing part of his knife to whack the window. It didn't break on the first hit but he tried again and this time it cracked. He kicked it with his foot and it exploded outward, raining safety glass onto the road.

The werewolf lost control of the van and it careened into a ditch lining the road. As this happened, James reached his arm through the broken window and pressed the latch to open the door.

The door popped open as the van tilted to the side, coming to a stop. All three boys rolled across the floor and the werewolf managed to grab on to Kyle's cape.

"He's got me! The werewolf's got me!" Kyle yelled, the terror in his voice apparent. "Help me, guys!"

James crawled over to Kyle and used his Swiss Army knife to cut the cape a few inches from the werewolf's hand. Falling free, Kyle scrambled to the open van door.

"Come here, ya little brats!" the werewolf yelled as he tried to untie himself so he could chase the boys. All three boys jumped out of the van and began running for their lives down the dark road.

They didn't stop until they were more than a quarter mile from the van, each of them breathing hard and gasping for air.

"What do we do now?" Kyle asked, his voice barely a whisper. James was about to reply when headlights lit up the night and all three boys screamed in fear.

"He's back! The werewolf found us!" Richard yelled as he shielded his eyes from the glare of the headlights.

"What are you boys doing out here all alone?" a voice called to them. James knew instantly it wasn't the werewolf.

As the owner of the voice began to walk out of the headlights, and James could see the person better, he saw the reflection of a policeman's badge. And when he squinted some more, he saw the vehicle wasn't a van but a squad car.

They were saved!

The policeman looked up as another vehicle approached them. All three boys turned to look and saw it was the beat-up van, the werewolf behind the wheel. When the werewolf saw the policeman, he continued past them, only slowing enough to glare at James.

The policeman chuckled when he saw the driver of the van. "Huh, Halloween, gotta love it, huh, boys? He must be going to a party."

None of the boys said anything until the policeman looked at them once more. "So, I'll ask again, what are you kids doing all the way out here?"

James shrugged, and with as calm a voice as he could muster, he said, "Nothing much. We were walking and got lost is all. Can you give us a ride to Third Street, sir?"

The officer scratched his forehead and sighed. "I'm not a cab service, son, but yes, this one time I will. It's not safe out here in the dark and I don't want you boys getting into trouble. Hop in," he said and ushered the boys into the squad car.

Once they were all inside and on their way, James looked at Kyle and Richard. The policeman was in front of them in the driver's seat, and with the plastic barrier separating him from them, he couldn't hear what James was saying.

"We make a promise right here and now that we never talk about what happened tonight, all right?" James said in a hushed tone.

"Who would believe us anyway? Hell, I was there and I still don't believe it." Richard said.

"You made me lose my cross," Kyle said. "My mom's gonna kill me."

"Better a hypothetical one than a real one, Kyle," James huffed.

The boys remained silent for the rest of the ride. When the squad pulled over at the top of Third Street and the officer climbed out and opened the back door for the kids to leave, he waggled a finger at them and said, "Now, you boys stay out of trouble, ya hear?"

"Believe me, sir, we will," James said as they began to walk down the street. "Thank you for the ride."

The officer was soon distracted when a few new trick-or-treaters walked by him and he chatted with the parents of the children.

James led the way to the first house, and just before he reached the door, his cell phone rang. Opening it, he said, "Hello?"

"James? It's Mom, I just wanted to check on you. Are you okay?"

"I'm fine, Mom, I'm on Third Street. I should be home in a half hour."

"Okay, just stay safe. And remember, no talking to people you don't know."

He chuckled then. "What about werewolves? Can I talk to them?"

"What? Are you trying to be funny?"

"Yes, Mom, that's exactly what I'm trying to do. Don't worry, I'll be fine."

"Okay, talk to you when you get home." She hung up and James put the phone away.

Richard and Kyle returned from the front door of the house and Kyle handed James a big candy bar. "Here, I got you one, too."

"Thanks," James said. "So, are we gonna finish getting candy or what?"

"You bet," Richard said, feeling better now that they were safe and everything was back to normal. He turned and began walking down the path, leaving Kyle and James alone for a second. As they stood side by side, other children walked by them, going to get candy from the home owner.

James turned to look at his friend, who did the same to him.

"So werewolves really exist, who knew?" Kyle asked.

"Yeah, who knew," James repeated as the two boys began walking, quickly catching up with Richard who was already at the next house.

None of the three boys ever spoke of the events of that night, especially when the next day, four children were reported missing, all of them vanishing without a trace while trick-or-treating.

James wanted to tell the police what he and his friends knew, but he was positive that no one would believe him.

But James knew that next Halloween, when the moon was full, he was going to be on the lookout for a battered old van with a werewolf in the driver's seat.

And if he found it, well, Batman was a superhero after all, and the werewolf was a villain.

The rest would work itself out.

THE BIG SURPRISE

HOPE YANDELL

Only one more night to go and we would be out begging for candy. Houses were decorated with long strands of orange lights. Jack o' lanterns leered at us as Keegan and I ran down the dark street in anticipation of Halloween. One small house near the end of our street had a ghost in their side yard that drifted between trees along an invisible wire. I watched the dark phantom limp behind the biggest tree thinking, *I hope there's a wire holding that thing up*. The cold air from the nearby swamp made me shiver as we hurried past the last of the holiday decorations in search of adventure.

My best friend Keegan told me it would be 'cool' to go into the graveyard next to a deserted Methodist church in our trick-or-treat costumes. Personally, I was afraid and told her 'no.' Then she double-dared me to do it, so here I am, dressed up as Catwoman in a neglected cemetery with Keegan who is dressed up as a vampire. A graveyard is in second place on my top ten list of freaky places I would hate to go. First place belongs to haunted houses, which is our next destination.

We were walking around a broken headstone, when Keegan pointed out Miss Manatee's old house. The elderly lady moved out last month. She said the house was too big for one person to take care of and no one had ever moved in so the sprawling mansion was abandoned. The spooky mansion reminded me of a haunted house in a scary movie. As we neared the sinister home, dark windows stared at us in silent eagerness. My heart beat faster and I slowed to a stop, staring back.

Keegan grabbed my arm and dragged me over to the house saying, "Come on chicken! Let's go check it out."

She should know me better than that. I pulled my arm free to lead the way saying, "No one calls me chicken."

We walked slowly towards the frightening home, but as we became closer and closer, the house looked spookier and spookier. I began to feel even more afraid. Finally, we reached a rusty metal gate that opened onto a narrow cobblestone path leading to the front door of Miss Manatee's house. I wished we were back home, or at least back at the cemetery, because even it wasn't this spooky. The dead things buried there stayed dead. I wasn't sure that held true in this place.

The house and its property looked like the church cemetery. In the old days, some families would bury their loved ones near their home. This was one of the old plantation houses in the area that predated the Civil War.

There were gravestones from the old family burial ground scattered everywhere in the front yard, behind the wrought iron gate and fence. A nearby stable and barn were part of the original plantation as was the house. The slave's quarters burned down one Halloween night a year before I was born. My dad told me you could hear screams coming from the old building as fires consumed it, but no bodies were ever found. He believed it must have been the wind howling through the trees or tom cats fighting that sounded like people screaming.

We opened the squeaky gate and started down the path. Big, black bats flew through the air above me. One even swooped down so low that it nearly hit my head! I kept hearing odd noises like groans and moans. Every time I heard a noise, I kept telling myself, *it's just the wind*, or *come on get yourself together; it's just my imagination playing tricks on me.*

At last, we reached the front door. I told Keegan we should leave because old houses can be dangerous. That was true, but I wasn't going to admit the real reason I wanted to leave was because I was so scared. All of my friends told me spooky stories about this house and said Miss Manatee really left because the house is haunted. Even teenagers stayed away from here.

That is why my, *soon to be deceased if anything goes wrong*, best friend bet I would chicken out and not go inside. She was almost right, but like I said, *nobody calls me chicken.*

Keegan appeared to have second thoughts, too, after we climbed the broken concrete steps to the flimsy wooden porch.

She said, "Okay, okay we'll go back home, but it isn't because I'm afraid. It's because we could get hurt or something."

There was a loud *bang* that came from the graveyard and it scared me half to death.

I looked around in time to see a shadowy figure move from behind a headstone near the gate. He was stooped over and dragged one leg behind him as if he was injured. The man reminded me of the shadowy ghost we saw hiding behind the tree at the small house near the end of our street.

We ran back to the mansion. Keegan was going to run inside without waiting to see if anyone was in there, but I stopped her to let her know that we should at least ring the doorbell. My mom and dad were super-strict when it came to respecting people's homes and this had to be a joke of some kind.

Didn't it?

When Keegan pulled the antique chime, it sounded like an old foghorn I've heard at night near our vacation home on Hilton Head Island when the weather turns bad. Cold chills tickled my spine. I looked through the grime-covered windows to see shadows moving in the hall. It was too dark and the window was too dirty to see what was making them. Nobody answered the door, and then there was another loud *bang* from behind us, but this one sounded scarier and louder than the first one. The door was unlocked so we just ran straight inside without worrying about our good manners this time.

I hurried to close the door and hit the light switch. These aged lights aren't as bright as the ones in modern homes. Everything got a smidge less dark, but the flickering bulbs were still too dim to drive all the shadows away. We heard noises coming from upstairs. They were loud noises, like an army marching, so we argued about going up there until someone struck the door behind us. Then whoever or whatever it was jiggled the doorknob.

Keegan snatched my hand and yelled, "Follow me!"

We hurried up the steps, forgetting about all the fears we had before.

Our feet went, *thud, thud, thud*, as we ran up the wooden stairs. As soon as we were at the top of the staircase, we heard the noises again but this time it sounded like laughs, and small giggles. I was totally freaked out! Keegan nudged me from behind. As soon as I gathered up my courage, I led her to the source of the noises, which was behind a big brown door.

I slowly opened it...

"*SURPRISE!*" everyone screamed, including Keegan, and then people jumped out of their hiding places.

It was a big surprise party for me!

I totally forgot, today was my thirteenth birthday! As impossible as that seems, I had been so caught up in the Halloween festivities with my family and friends that I lost track of time. My mom and dad came over to greet me with a hug. Keegan's parents and her little sister, Melissa, was here, too. Our other best friends Shelly and Morgan were here also, along with our neighbors, the Gonzales'. Everyone was dressed up for the holidays and to have fun, except my big brother, Chris.

I thought to myself, *That must be who scared us out front. I bet he followed us from town and did that to make sure we wouldn't change our minds about coming inside or going upstairs.* I noticed the sound of something scraping along the floor in the hall growing louder. I gave dad a wink and smile. "Here comes Chris!" I yelled.

Dad looked at Mom in confusion. "Is Chris going to be here?"

Chris has a busy social life and he hasn't come to any of my birthday parties since he moved out of the house five years ago. This was going to be the biggest and best surprise ever.

A loud hammering at the large brown door made everyone stop talking and look at it. I ran over to let my big brother inside.

Just as I turned the doorknob, I heard my mom say, "Chris text messaged me over an hour ago to say he can't make it."

Then the lights went out.

The End?

RIP

CHILDREN SHOULDN'T PLAY WITH DEAD THINGS

DAVID RENFROW

The sun was setting, losing its nightly battle with the coming darkness. An October chill permeated the air, and all the children who were made to wear coats over their Halloween costumes, pulled the thick collars a little tighter.

The streets were alive and crawling with groups of children going door to door, begging for sugary treats. Here and there mixed in with the crowds, impatient parents attempted to control goblins and wizards running around in circles.

Mark Jessup and his two friends, Rebecca and Jason Short—they were twins—stood separated from the rest of the sugar-fueled revelers. At fourteen, Mark and Jason thought they were too cool to trick-or-treat. They preferred instead to spend the early part of the evening shaking down unaccompanied little kids for candy, before beginning the real work of egging and toilet-papering the rest of the neighborhood, long after the younger children were in bed.

Mark lay on the hood of an abandoned car, eating a peanut butter cup. He was pudgy, with hair slicked back and a cheap plastic monster mask on top of his head. A fresh chocolate stain covered the already dirty t-shirt he wore with a ripped pair of blue jeans.

"Man, I'm bored," Rebecca whined. "We've already got enough candy; can't we go and find something exciting to do?"

Mark snickered while Jason looked at his sister and rolled his eyes. "Geez, Rebecca," Jason said from the hood of the car where he sat next to Mark. "You're never happy."

"Shut up, Jason, I just don't wanna sit here all night," she snapped.

Mark reached deep into his sack of candy. "You know, Jason, she may have a point. This place is pretty boring right now. Maybe we should find something better to do." He exchanged a sly smirk with Jason, who smiled back.

"Yeah, maybe you're right, Mark. Maybe it's time that we take Rebecca up to the cemetery."

The boys could see their conversation had an immediate effect on Rebecca.

"What cemetery?" she asked.

"Well," Mark replied. "A few weeks ago, your brother and I were exploring those woods up near the town line, and we came across an old abandoned cemetery. It looks like it's been there since like the Puritans or something."

"Wow," Rebecca said quietly. "That sounds kind of cool. But you really think it's a good idea to go poking around some old cemetery in the dark, on Halloween night?"

The boys laughed, causing Rebecca to blush. She didn't want the boys to think she was a coward.

"Well," Jason answered, "I mean, if you're not up to it than you're not up to it. Come on, Mark, we'll go up there ourselves."

The boys jumped off the car and started to walk away from Rebecca.

"Hey!" she called out. "Don't leave, I wanna see it." She ran and caught up with the boys.

Jason put his arm around his slightly taller sister. "Glad you decided to join us, sis. Trust me, you won't be sorry."

* * *

Working their way across town, it took them fifteen minutes to arrive at the old cemetery. They paused at the gate, which was covered in clinging ivory and climbing tree vines.

Mark looked at Rebecca and asked, "You sure you're ready for this, kid?"

"First of all," she answered snidely, "Jason and I are three months older than you. Second of all, I'm not scared. I just want to make sure this is a good idea." She took a deep breath. "Yeah, I'm ready, so let's do this." She pushed past the two boys and walked into the old cemetery.

The light gray of twilight, had given way to the inky blackness of night. Mark pulled out a small flashlight and handed it to Rebecca before pulling out a second one for himself.

"Man, this place is so cool," Jason whispered.

Mark laughed. "Why you whispering, you dork?"

Jason shifted uncomfortably, "I don't know. I just don't want anyone to hear us. I can't get in anymore trouble this month."

Mark shined his flashlight down on the nearest grave, "Trust me, dude, I think anyone who might hear us probably won't care that we're here."

The trio walked for five minutes. But out here in the middle of the gravestones, it felt like they had been walking forever.

"Where are we going, anyways? What are we looking for?" Rebecca asked, trying to catch her breath.

Mark pointed further into the darkness. "There's this old crypt up here that we want to take a look at, but couldn't the last time we were up here."

"You mean, we're gonna go into a crypt? Like where they keep dead bodies?"

"That's the plan," Jason answered without looking at her. He was more interested in reading the gravestones they were passing by. "Hey, look at this one, guys." His light reflected dimly against the worn rock. "It says, 'John Simpson 1700-1754. Died during the great Flu outbreak'. Wow that's pretty cool that they put how he died."

"Yeah," Rebecca said, "they used to do that all the time back in the old days."

Mark shined his light in her eyes. "You read too many books, Rebecca."

She stuck her tongue out at him. "Maybe you should pick one up every once and a while. Maybe then you'd be in the grade you're supposed to be in."

Mark raised his arm, like he was going to throw his flashlight right at Rebecca, but Jason's flashlight beam reflected off the glass of an ancient and long forgotten crypt. "Hey, guys, look, there it is."

"Wow," Mark said excitedly, "and it's open. We can get in."

As they approached the small iron and concrete structure, Rebecca again voiced her concerns. "You guys really think it's a good idea to go in there?"

"Yes, Rebecca," Mark said sarcastically as he stepped into the crypt. "Nothing's going to get us, I promise. You just have to learn to..."

Suddenly Mark's light bounced off something in the crypt. He screamed as he fell back, knocking Rebecca and Jason off the stone stairs.

"What's going on?" Jason yelled. He picked up Mark's dropped flashlight and swept the beam into the crypt. "Mark, you're such a jerk. It's just a stone gargoyle."

Mark stood up and dusted himself off. "Are you sure?" he asked hesitatingly. "I thought I saw it move."

Jason started laughing as he kept the light on the unmoving stone figure. "Yeah, I'm sure. There's nothing in here."

"All right," Mark said, taking charge again of his emotions. "Let's check this place out."

It was cramped in the crypt, with no room for the three to really move around. The walls had large cracks in them that had allowed water to pool on the hard cement floor. The entire crypt reeked of mold and decay. The three kids looked at the stone coffin dead center of the room. Rebecca reached out slowly to touch the lid.

"Boo!" Mike yelled, causing Rebecca to jump back.

"You're such a jerk," she said angrily, preparing to punch Mark.

"Wow, easy there, girl," Jason said quietly as he reached out to grab his sister's arm before she could swing at Mark.

"Should we open it?" Mark directed the question at Jason.

Jason shook his head slowly before responding. "No, I think we should probably just leave it alone. Too much bad mojo for me."

Mark looked at the twins, the disgust evident in his young but tough face. "Fine you two. You're both pansies. Let's go check out some more of those grave stones outside."

They had to duck as they left, and pull the spider webs out of their hair. They walked deeper into the old cemetery. Mark picked up a branch and touched Rebecca's shoulder. Her scream cut through the night as she jumped.

"What are you doing, you jerk? Don't do that!"

The two boys looked at each other and laughed.

"Relax, Becca. Didn't know that you were gonna throw a tantrum," Mark laughed.

"You two are juvenile delinquents. You better knock it off, Jason, or I'm gonna tell Mom." The two boys just continued to laugh. "Fine, then I'm leaving." She turned to stalk off, but before she could take one step, the three of them felt the ground shake.

"What was that?" Mark yelled. The shaking continued and the three kids fell to the dirt, dropping their candy bags, which spilled open next to them. Miniature candy bars and peanut butter cups rolled off in all directions. The ground all around the three ripped open and shifted, forcing them to reach out and hold on to the ancient tombstones or risk falling into the gaping holes.

Suddenly, from one of the holes, a rotting, leathery hand reached out. It grabbed at the surrounding tree debris and pulled. Rebecca screamed as the long dead corpse emerged from its slumber and grabbed onto Jason's legs and began pulling him into its plot. Rebecca reached out for her brother's hand, gripping it tightly, and pulled as hard as she could.

"Mark!" she yelled. "Help me pull him back!"

Mark continued to look at Rebecca and then back at the zombie in utter shock. This couldn't be real. These things didn't happen in real life, only in the movies. "Mark, you have to help me! It's going to kill Jason!" she yelled.

Mark's look of shock was replaced by one of confusion and then finally he jumped from where he'd fallen and grabbed Jason by the shoulders.

"Rebecca, pull harder! This thing is really strong!" Mark commanded.

The zombie screamed and pulled even harder on Jason's legs, who kicked his feet, striking the horrible corpse in the face. Something to the side of her caused Rebecca to look up suddenly while she was pulling. A second zombie was emerging from another grave. It was a woman this time, wearing a threadbare dress, hair filled with worms, and sunken eyes. The female zombie reached out towards Mark.

"Mark, look out!" she screamed. But it was too late. The zombie reached out her long arms and grabbed Mark by the hair, lifting him off the ground. Mark struggled, but the zombie was just too strong. Rebecca watched as the original zombie dragged Jason into the soft earth, and the woman disappeared with Mark into the darkness of her own grave.

The ground shifted beneath Rebecca again, and with a scream on her lips, she ran out of the cemetery. She didn't want to be sitting there when the next hungry zombie escaped. With the sounds of Mark's and Jason's screams carrying through the night air, she aimed for the lights of downtown, and didn't stop running until she got there, having no idea how to explain what had happened to her brother and her friend.

HALLOWEEN DREAMER

DAVID FRENCH

Emily sat with her younger brother Todd on the side of his bed in their new house. They were sad.

It was the morning of Halloween 1934 and their father had gotten a new job working on a large bridge in California. The family had to move suddenly, and this meant leaving their friends and family behind for many years.

To make matters worse, it was Emily's twelfth birthday.

The children had just finished unpacking their suitcases after the long trip to California, when their mom called them down for lunch. Being Emily's birthday, her mom made things better by running out and getting some cake and ice cream at the store; this helped cheer them up a lot.

As they finished the last few bites, their mother reminded them, "Don't go into the attic, those things up there belong to someone else. We don't know who they are, but they're supposed to be here tomorrow." No sooner had she finished, then Emily and her eight year old brother took off running upstairs, shouting, "Okay, we *won't*!"

"What are you going out as?" Todd asked as he headed to his room.

"I think I'll go as a witch," Emily said.

Todd looked at his feet as he stopped in the doorway, then back up to his sister. "I wish dad was here," he said sadly.

Emily smiled big, and replied, "So do I, then he could have unpacked all those boxes!" Still smiling, she ran into her room to put on her costume.

A few minutes later, Todd met Emily in the hall, and she saw he was dressed as a pirate, as unusual.

"Let's go into the attic and see what's up there," she said. Emily had a devilish smile on her face, knowing that she was about to have some harmless fun. Todd's eyes grew big and his mouth puckered up in the thought of doing something wrong; he never did anything wrong on his own.

"There's probably swords and daggers and who knows what else up there," she said with a sly grin.

"Okay, but if I get into trouble, I'm blaming you," he said and rushed to his sister's side.

Once in the attic, they were amazed at the collection of strange and unusual artifacts that lined the walls of the small area.

Large, unopened crates with foreign stampings on their sides, golden Egyptian's busts, and wooden carvings, were stacked in the corners. Paintings of strange lands and frightening faces hung from the rafters, and so much more. With so much to see, they forgot to be quiet.

Emily opened a drawer to an old desk that was in the center of the attic. She felt around in the drawer, and just as her mother entered the attic, she grabbed a cube-shaped object.

"I told you two this stuff isn't ours! I can't believe you two! Get to your rooms right now!" Mom said as she watched the two of them go down the ladder.

In her bedroom, Emily wasn't happy at being caught, but she held onto the object she had found in the old desk. It felt cold in the palm of her hand, like it had a life of its own.

"I'm disappointed that you went into the attic after I said not to," her mother said. "And you took Todd; you know he'll do whatever you tell him to do." Her mother shook her head and left the bedroom. Then she stopped in the hall and looked back at Emily who was mad at being chastised. She made a silent wish that her mother would leave her alone.

"Now you get ready to take Todd out for Halloween. Don't go far and don't get into anymore trouble!" She walked away.

Emily, now alone, held the cubed-shaped object up to the light. It was shiny and black. It looked like some kind of a stone.

It had four even corners, and she saw it had strange markings on its six flat surfaces.

She could feel that it was colder than it had been before.

With all the stress of moving and unpacking, she felt herself becoming tired, and she fell asleep. Her arms gently fell to her sides, and in her left hand, she gently held the small cube.

* * *

Her eyes opened with a start, as if she were late for school!

Looking around the room, she was confused.

Wait, this isn't my room! I was just in my room, where am I? she wondered.

She looked at her clothes, and saw she was still wearing her witch's costume. Rising from the bed, she began to walk in this unfamiliar place; everything was so strange. When she went outside, she saw the neighborhood she'd known was gone, replaced by buildings she didn't recognize.

A man came along and he was walking very fast. "Oh, hello, little witch. I've never seen you before." He stopped and tipped his tall hat to her with a polite smile.

He was dressed oddly, but it is Halloween, she figured.

"Where am I?" she asked him. *I must be dreaming*, she thought. But everything felt real and she was beginning to get worried, dream or not!

The strange man turned away and started walking again.

"Wait, where are you going?" Emily ran to keep up with him. "I really do need to get home, my mother will be worried," she told him.

"No one goes home from here, little witch." He pushed the knee high grass out of his way with his cane as he quickly walked along past the buildings and into a field.

They soon came to a low hill top. Behind them was tall grass, and in front of them was a field of short flowers. They were beautiful and full of colors.

There were tall trees full of bright green leaves on either side of a path that seemed to disappear into the horizon.

Emily was beginning to become frightened that she was lost.

"I'm scared, can't you help me? Where are we going?"

The tall strange man looked down at her. "I'll help you, little witch, just follow me."

They started walking again and they entered the path of trees.

The trees were so thick they blocked the sky and made the path dark.

"You've never told me your name, mine's Emily."

The tall strange man looked puzzled. "I don't remember my name." He looked sad as he said this.

Emily started walking towards the trees as the man was thinking. He turned to see the young girl getting too close to a tree. "*Stop*!" he shouted, but she was already too close.

The tree slapped a thin branch at her, hitting her hard on the left arm. She felt the pain where the tree struck her and she fell hard to the ground, putting a slight cut on her right hand. "How can this be? You're not supposed to feel pain in a dream," she said.

Emily was on her feet at once and ran to the tall man as another branch reached out and missed her, but managed to rip her costume.

"What was that? Trees that attack people, who ever heard of such things?"

"I can tell you're not from here, but neither was I at one time. You don't go near these trees, they don't like people. They were put here by one of the genies." He started walking again.

"How many genies are there?" Emily asked in a meek voice.

He replied in a jolly voice. "Two." He waved two fingers in the air.

Eyes began to appear on the trees, and thousands of trees watched the two travelers as they made their way down the path.

"If you're to survive here, you will have to learn a lot," he said. "When we reach the next town, I'll take you to someone that will teach you everything you need to know. She taught me well and look at me, I'm still alive."

When Emily didn't come down to take Todd out for Halloween, her mother went upstairs. She found Emily in bed barely breathing and unresponsive.

They were new in town and didn't know anyone yet and the phone hadn't been connected yet as they had just moved in. "Todd!" her mother cried. "Run next door and get someone to call a doctor...and hurry!"

Not far away was a gentleman named Stanley Poole, a professor and the foremost collector of unknown oddities. He had lived in Emily's house for more than a year until he had moved into a bigger home to have room for his private laboratory and his experiments.

No one had traveled as far as the professor and seen as much of the unknown world as he had. In his coat pocket, he was carrying an identical cube to the one Emily was holding. He didn't know that Emily had found the other one as he had lost it but didn't know it was missing...at least not yet.

When the professor purchased the cubes many years ago in Asia, he was told they belonged to twin sisters.

The sisters were said to be witches and it was said they had been trapped forever in the cubes for the crimes they committed. It was said that the two sisters would roll the cubes—really large dice—to determine the fate of people that crossed them—and sometimes things more sinister than death happened to these people!

Some legends say that the sisters were opposites, one good and the other evil!

Professor Poole was warned to never let the two dice come in contact with each other, for who knew what the sisters would do when together again!

He would sometimes sleep with one of the dice near him at night, and he would have dreams of a strange world. After a while he came to know this dream world and its inhabitants well enough to paint what he saw in his dreams.

On this Halloween night, Professor Poole felt his dice turn cold as ice in his pocket, and he knew its twin had been used. Reaching into his pocket, he was surprised to only see one of the dice. That was when he knew he'd misplaced the other one and knew it could only be in one place—Emily's house.

This was very bad news, for someone to use one of the dice and not understand how it worked could be very dangerous. Dropping what he was doing, he rushed to his former home as the street lights came on outside.

Emily's fears grew as the path narrowed and the angry trees grew closer to the two travelers.

In the distance, a girl's laughter could be heard; Emily looked toward the sound.

"Don't look, it's temptation calling us," the man said.

She couldn't help it and she looked anyway, her curiosity getting the better of her.

Ghostly images appeared in the forest.

"Come play with us," one called from behind the trees. "The trees won't harm you if you're with us," softly spoke another unseen creature in the dark.

Emily's fears rose sharply as the haunting voices called to her. The path narrowed more and became dangerous to traverse. The trees lashed out wildly at them and the ghostly temptations moved close enough to touch.

The tall man swung his cane at the thin branches as the angry trees attacked them.

The ghostly beings reached for Emily, trying to pull her into the forest.

The tall man picked her up and started running down the path. It was now so thin that his feet were wider than it.

"Our fates are intertwined now, if you die I die, little witch!" he said.

Emily closed her eyes and held on. She opened them as they reached a wooden bridge. The tall man put her down and took a much needed deep breath.

"I haven't had that much fun in years," he said with a wide grin. "You aren't hurt, are you, little witch?"

"I'm not hurt, and my name is Emily. And you've never told me yours."

"It has been too long since I used it, I can't remember." He looked down at the wooden bridge and started to walk away deep in thought.

Emily turned back to see the forest was quiet again, the leaves swaying gently in the breeze as if never disturbed, the trees immobile once more.

She wondered if it had all been her imagination.

Professor Poole knocked calmly on the front door of his former house, his heart racing in fear.

Todd answered the door with big eyes, and upon seeing the man before him, Todd assumed it was the doctor for Emily.

"Come in, it's my sister, she's upstairs. Please help her!" The frightened child was crying.

With a heavy European accent, Professor Poole asked to be taken to the room Emily was in.

Emily's mother was holding her right hand. "Oh, Doctor, I'm so glad you're here. She's not well."

"There's been a mistake, I'm Professor Poole. This was my house before you and I believe I left something here of the utmost importance. I believe this young girl may have found an object that looks similar to this." From his coat pocket he produced the singular dice.

Emily's mother was about to get angry, when he held up a hand.

"It is this dice that I believe made your child ill."

"What are you talking about?"

"Never mind how," Professor Poole said. "Just help me find the dice. That is how we can help her!"

"I've seen this place! I saw it in a painting in my attic!" Emily spun around while looking at everything. "Yes! And you, too. I saw a painting of you!"

The tall man shook his head. "I know nothing of what you speak, little witch."

Looking into the water from up on the bridge, she saw frightening creatures swimming back and forth; these too she had seen in the paintings.

"Come, we will be in the town soon, and I will take you to the sorceress."

Emily's mother raised the girl's left hand hidden in the sheets and the dice fell out and landed heavily on the wooden floor. Professor Poole picked up the dice and placed one in his left pocket and the other in his right.

"Good, now that I have recovered the dice, give me some time and I'll do my best to help!" he said as he left the room. "She should be fine if all goes well."

There was a second knock at the door, and this time Todd returned with the doctor.

The doctor opened his bag and went to work on the girl, not understanding why she was unconscious.

Downstairs, the professor was busy rolling the dice.

At the same time, Emily's mother was sitting by the bed holding her daughter's hand.

As Emily and the tall man approached the town, they heard lively music playing and happy voices singing.

They entered the town and Emily was amazed at all of the activity! The walls of the buildings that lined the crowded streets were painted with scenes from around the world, *her world*.

Emily turned and looked up at the tall man. "Where are these places that are painted on the walls and who painted them?" she asked.

"I don't know," he replied. "They have always been there."

"You have lived here so long that you have forgotten your name and yet you've never been to these places!" she said.

The tall man looked down at her, not saying a word.

"Where were you coming from when we met?" Her heart was beating a little faster.

"It doesn't matter," he said. "We should go and see the sorceress now." He began to walk away from her again. She followed closely behind him not wanting to lose the only person she knew in this strange world.

"I don't know what's wrong," the doctor stated as he moved across the room. "She seems to be asleep and wont wake up, and her heart keeps speeding up and slowing down. Other than that there's nothing else I can find wrong with her. I've done all I can, but I'll stay with her until the morning." He settled into a small chair next to the window.

Downstairs, Professor Poole was still rolling the dice, but he never let the two touch.

"This is it," the tall man said.

They stopped in front of a small sign that read, **FORTUNES TOLD!**

"This is where I leave you..." He started to say little witch, but stopped himself. "Good luck, Emily." He didn't wait for her to reply as he quickly walked away, leaving Emily to stand alone.

Climbing the three steps to the door that led into the business of the sorceress was scary, but she hoped that this was her way home. The door was small, and a tiny bell rang as she opened it.

"I've been waiting for you, dear." The female voice seemed very loud in the small, dark room.

"Do me a favor child, close your eyes and try to relax. Think of the largest place you've ever been in, and think of something that makes you happy." Emily did this, and the woman smiled.

"Now open your eyes slowly," the woman said calmly.

As Emily opened her eyes, the room became huge, and well lit.

"That's much better, thank you. Please don't be frightened anymore. It's *your* fears and thoughts that influence my home."

Emily moved closer, but she kept her distance from the mysterious woman behind the table.

"How is this possible? This place isn't real," Emily said and waved her arms calmly.

"Well, you are somewhat right, it isn't real, but you control what is here with your thoughts alone."

Emily looked at the throbbing cut on her right hand from where a branch had whacked her and saw blood. That was real.

"Concentrate and make the wound heal, dear," the woman said.

Emily closed her eyes and wished the cut away. When she opened her eyes again, it was gone. Not so much as a scar remained.

"You don't belong here, child, you're not a real witch. Why would dress like a witch and use the dice?" the woman asked.

"I didn't know what it was, this is all a mistake," Emily said. She suddenly found herself incredibly tired and she yawned loudly.

"Here, child, come lay down for a bit, you do look tired," the woman said.

Emily was led to a small bed where she plopped down without taking off her shoes. She was sleeping a second later.

Emily's mother let go her of her daughter's right hand as Emily began to mouth words, but they were so low her mother couldn't make them out.

"Doctor, she's waking up I think!"

The doctor turned to look at Emily and stood up. He sat on the bed next to her and listened to her heart. "Her heart is calming, becoming steadier. Give her some time, I think everything will be all right by morning." He went back to his chair and watched her.

"I hope you're right, Doctor," Emily's mother said as she caressed Emily's cheek with her left hand. "I don't know what I would ever do without her."

"Be glad my sister didn't get you, or you would be here forever little *want to be witch*!" the woman said as Emily's drifted off to sleep.

Emily heard her mother's voice singing softly to her and she opened her eyes.

"Mom?" Emily said as she slowly woke up. She looked at the doctor and then back to her mother. "I dreamt I was in another world." She looked over to the doorway and there was the man that had taken her to the sorcer-ess.

Professor Poole was much older in the real world, but she recognized him immediately.

She was about to speak to the professor, but Todd got between them.

"I'll be here tomorrow and you can tell me every-thing." The professor said with a smile. "For now you need to rest."

Emily's mother kissed her on the forehead and every-one left her alone, the doctor talking to her mother as they left the room.

"We're still going trick-or-treating, right?" Todd asked Emily.

"You bet we are," she said happily. He skipped away, happy for the coming night. He planned on eating so much candy he would be sick for a week.

As she lay in bed and stared up at the ceiling, she re-called her dream, and though she tried to tell herself it was a dream, when she looked down at her witch's cos-tume and saw the large rip where a tree had tried to grab her, she realized that her Halloween adventure had been real.

THE CREATURE FROM HOYT BOTTOM

TERRY ALEXANDER

Crimson ribbons streaked the western sky, burning scarlet on the high cottony clouds. An early evening chill settled with the deepening twilight.

Everyone gathered at Davey's cabin, outside the small community of Hoyt, Oklahoma, near the South Canadian River. The kids jostled around an immense pile of logs, waiting for the proper moment to touch off the bonfire. Davey scraped a match along the wood and held it to the tinder. The flames ate into the paper kindling and spread into the smaller pieces of shaved pine.

"Story time! Gather around, it's story time." Davey sipped at a cold Cherry RC. "Has anyone got any good Halloween stories before the hayride?"

"Are we going to the river bottoms?" a young freckled-faced girl with red hair asked.

"No," Davey answered quickly. "Not the river bottom. Nobody goes to the bottoms after dark." His face paled. "Now, someone give us a story," he said, quickly changing the subject.

Several youngsters and teenagers raised their hands, ready to tell some whoppers.

For the next hour, half a dozen variations of Jason, Freddy and Michael Meyers' stories were told, and then a hush fell over the circle.

"What about you, Tom?" Davey asked as he sat on a lawn chair near the fire. "You're always good for a story."

A dark clad man glanced up from the flames, his long gray hair in a pony tail. He pushed his baseball cap—sporting a feed store emblem—back on his head. Shaking a cigarette from his pack, he lit it with a flaming ember. "Anyone ever heard of Mike Cooper, the creature of Hoyt bottom?"

"Lame," a single voice sounded from the back of the circle.

Tom ignored the comment as a wry smile crossed his face. "It happened on Halloween night five years ago. Winter came in early, a cold wind blowing in from Canada, putting everyone in heavy coats." A cloud of smoke obscured his face. "We were on a hayride. Mike Cooper waited out on one of the dirt roads to the river bottom. The plan was simple. Curt Jennings was going to stop at a marked spot along the road and shine a spotlight on Mike. Mike was supposed to slip a green Frankenstein mask over his face and yell and scream like a banshee and scare the tar out of the kids."

"I remember. I was on that hayride," Davey nodded.

Tom threw his cigarette into the fire. "Then everything went wrong."

* * *

Mike Cooper shivered in a small grove of elm trees twenty feet off the gravel road. A cold wind whipped through his light jacket and chilled him to the bone. His arms were folded across his chest to conserve body heat.

Where are they? he wondered.

He looked through the darkness toward the curve, a quarter mile up the road, hoping to spot the glare of approaching headlights.

He pushed the button on a small flashlight to check the time, then fished his pocket watch from his jeans. Wrist watches didn't run when Mike wore them, something about the natural electricity in his body messing them up.

They should have been here fifteen minutes ago.

He breathed a little easier when twin hi-beams swept around the curve.

About time. A man could freeze to death out here, he thought.

A spotlight shined out of a harvested corn field a hundred yards from him, the broken stalks pointed at the night sky like obscene fingers.

What's Curt doing? He knows I'm in the trees.

The beam went dark, as the headlights drew closer.

That's got to be them. Curt must be trying to show the kids some deer. I can't wait till he stops, those kids are going to wet their pants when they see me.

The vehicle slowed.

Come on, Curt, just a little closer.

Mike bit his lip in anticipation. The pickup stopped. The spotlight hit the trees.

Showtime.

Mike fitted the mask over his head, covering his face, and jumped into the center of the light. A loud, blood-chilling roar ripped from his lips and his hands were held in the classic pose of the Frankenstein monster.

"What in the world is that?" The words came out slurred, a faint whiff of alcohol swirled in the wind.

Who's that? I don't know that voice, Mike wondered.

Chill bumps prickled the flesh along his arms.

"Keep the light on it," a large figure said as it stepped away from the pickup.

What's he holding?

Mike reached for the mask to remove it.

"Hurry up, Lane. There's a car coming."

Mike risked a quick glance up the road to see a second set of headlights rounding the curve.

"Oh my God," he mumbled. "Wait, hold on," he called as he tore the mask from his face. "Hold on."

Thunder exploded in the night. A bright red flash blinded him even as a sledgehammer blow slammed his chest, punching a hole through his back. Mike collapsed to his knees and flopped down on his back, his chest burning like fire.

"Get in, Lane! Get in, someone's coming!"

"I hit it. I want to see what it is."

"Forget it. We've got to get out of here," another voice said. The pickup's door slammed, then gravel sprayed, pinging off metal fenders.

Mike wheezed; he struggled to draw breath into his lungs. A warm sticky liquid flowed down his side. He tried to move but his limbs felt weighted, cemented to the ground.

"Mike! Mike! Are you okay?" Curt's voice sounded far away. "Mike, answer me."

Limbs and twigs snapped; a large shadow drew closer, a beam of light from a hand held light flashed over Mike's face, blinding him.

"Oh God, oh God. Cheryl, go to Dan Gardner's, call the sheriff and an ambulance!" Curt yelled.

"What's wrong? Is Mike hurt?"

"Just do what I said and hurry," Curt shouted. "I'm gonna stay here."

"Is he hurt?" Cheryl asked.

"Go, Cheryl!" Curt's voice grew louder. "Hurry."

Mike felt a hand close on his own. "Hang in there, Mike. Cheryl's gonna get help."

"I." The single word sent waves of agony coursing through Mike's body.

"Don't talk now, Mike. Help will be here in a few minutes. I'll stay right here with you. I won't leave you." Curt slipped his hand under Mike's back, applying pressure to staunch the flow of blood from the exit wound.

A cold sensation settled into Mike's feet, slowly creeping up his legs. "I'll get 'em. I'll get those two," he breathed, struggling with the words.

A rough hand brushed his hair back from his forehead. "Easy, buddy, just take it easy."

"I'll get 'em." Mike's eyelids drooped, his chin resting on his chest. "I need a little rest, just a little nap."

* * *

Probing hands broke Mike's slumber. An elastic band snapped on his ear; a mask settled over his face, jumbled bits of conversation filled his ears.

"His vital signs are weak."

"Look at that wound; had to be a 30-06."

"I need you to tell me everything you can about this."

"Not much to tell. We heard the shot and saw the taillights as the pickup pulled away."

"You sure it was a pickup?"

"It had to be. Poachers, probably."

Pain lanced through Mike's body. Dark, faceless shapes rolled him onto a stretcher. The cold vinyl drained the heat from his body as he settled into its welcoming embrace. Nylon straps tightened around his chest and extremities.

He felt a moment of weightlessness, of floating in the air.

"Take it easy. It's going to be tricky getting him out of this mess."

The flashing red and blue lights hurt his eyes.

"Get him stabilized. I'll get us to the hospital as fast as I can."

Mike's stretcher slid into the back of the ambulance. He stared up at the white, sterilized ceiling.

"Let's roll." The rear door of the ambulance slammed behind him. Mike closed his eyes, certain he'd wake up in the hospital.

* * *

"He died." An eight year old boy squatting near the fire broke the silence. "Mike died, didn't he?"

"Yes, boy, yes he did," Tom nodded.

"How did he become the creature if he died?" the boy asked.

Tom removed his ball cap, scratching an old scar near the hairline. "Well, I'll tell you. The police received a phone call of a break in at Martin's Funeral Home about four the next morning. Actually, it was more of a break out."

* * *

Mike opened his dead eyes. A dull, yellow glow burned within the orbs. Cold circulated within the room, the nylon straps bound him securely to the gurney. He glanced at his sterile surroundings, his mind a great empty void, only one thought remained behind his burning eyes.

Revenge.

He strained against his bonds, forcing his torso upright. The nylon cut into his flesh, slicing through skin and muscle like a sharp knife, cutting through to the bone. He felt no pain. He was beyond pain.

The stitching creaked and popped, snapping with a loud crack. With single-minded purpose, he tugged at the restraints on his legs. The strap shredded his fingers, small bits of skin and meat littered the floor. The strong material popped like a rifle shot.

Mike swung his legs to the floor. His tattered, blood-stained clothing hung loose on his frame. Stiff legs carried him to the door; his injured hands struck the steel frame.

After several failed attempts to smash it down, he accidentally turned the knob, opening the way to freedom. Starlight beckoned from the windows at the end of a long corridor. His shambling, lopsided gait carried him to the glass entryway. He struck the thick panes with open palms, pushing. He leaned in to the thick glass door, and pushed, with an unnatural strength. Cracks appeared in the thick panes, clear splinters rained down on the carpet. With a final effort, the glass burst outward.

He shambled outside; bits of glass stuck to his shuffling feet. His unsteady gait carried him along the sidewalk. He returned to Hoyt bottom.

* * *

"Martin's had video cameras mounted inside, in case anyone ever tried to break in. I saw the tape later," Tom said. "It was a poor quality, grainy, black and white VHS, of a man shattering the glass door from the inside. He stood there a moment, then his eyes focused on the camera, like he knew it was there. It was Mike Cooper, sure as anything,"

"Is he there now?" a young girl interrupted. "Down in the bottoms."

"Yes, he is." Tom shook another cigarette from his pack, using it as a pointer. "He wanders Hoyt bottom, searching for the men who killed him."

"How come no one has ever seen him?" a pimply faced teenager at the rear of the fire asked.

"Davey's seen him." Tom gazed over to the large man. "Haven't you?"

"Yeah, I saw him last spring," Davey said. His eyes sought the comfort of the fire. "I was fishing. It was a warm day and the water was low. I saw a man wading from the north bank toward me. The water had to be freezing. That's when the smell hit me." Davey's hands trembled. "It smelled like a dead cow was left out in the August heat for a week. My stomach rolled and I thought I was going to vomit." He paused to suck in a breath. "Things were falling off him, like rain drops sprinkling the water. The fish swarmed around him in a circle, darting around his legs and snatching up bits of meat. That's when I figured out the small things falling from him were maggots."

"During deer season a hunter named Vernon Carpenter was found dead in the woods by the river," Tom said, taking up the story. "Some one nearly ripped his arm off, and there were bits of dead skin imbedded around his throat, and under his fingernails. His family had him cremated the next day. I was always curious about that, it's like they wanted it over with fast." Tom lit another cigarette. "No one goes to the Canadian River bottoms at night anymore. Mike's still out there, but he's not Mike anymore.

He's the Creature from Hoyt Bottom."

WHICH IS WITCH?

REBECCA BESSER

"What's wrong?" Taylor Simmons asked as she walked up the porch steps, where her friend was sulking.

"Tiger went missing sometime yesterday," Susan Hughes said with a heavy sigh. "I've looked everywhere, but I still can't find him."

Sitting down, Taylor wrapped her arm around Susan and gave her a hug.

"How did he get out of the house? Don't you usually keep him inside?"

"Yeah," Susan said with a sniff. "Brian didn't shut the door when he took the trash out last night. It's the only time I know of that Tiger could have gotten out of the house."

"Maybe he'll come home on his own," Taylor said. "If he can't find food or something, maybe he'll just come back."

"But he doesn't have his claws," Susan sobbed softly. "What if he meets another cat and has to fight? He'll be at a disadvantage. Tomorrow is Halloween, what if someone does something mean to him just for fun? You know how boys can be!"

Taylor hugged her friend again. "How about we go for a walk around the block and see if we can find him, and if we don't, maybe one of our parents will drive us around to look for him later."

Susan sniffed, wiped tears from her cheeks, and nodded. "Dad said he would take me when he got home from work today, if it wasn't too dark."

Taylor smiled. "Hopefully we'll find Tiger and we won't have to worry about that."

Susan went in and told her mom what they planned to do.

When she came back outside, the two girls went for a walk to find the lost, orange, tiger-striped cat. Susan had gotten him for her tenth birthday, two years ago, and she was really attached to him.

They called his name and walked slowly, going to the door of each house to ask the residents if they had seen the cat. No one had.

"This is frustrating," Susan said. "He must have been seen by someone."

Soon, they came to Miss Nordstrom's house. She was a nice woman in her twenties who was friendly with the children of the neighborhood, always inviting them over for cookies or lemonade when she saw them outside playing. Not only was she friendly and nice, but she was beautiful as well. She had long blonde, curly hair, aqua blue eyes, and perfect white teeth. Her nose was the perfect size, and her dark pink lips were always smiling. The girls of the neighborhood always envied her and wanted to look just like her when they grew up.

The girls climbed the light-blue painted cement steps and smiled at each other as they rang the door bell. If anyone would help them, it would be Miss Nordstrom.

In a matter of moments, the door opened to the cheery smile the girls expected.

"Susan! Taylor!" Miss Nordstrom said happily. "What are you doing here? Come to visit? I just pulled a pumpkin roll out of the oven. Would you like to come in for a piece?"

The girls looked at each other, shrugged, and nodded yes. They could smell the pumpkin and spices in the air as it drifted out of the house, and it made them hungry.

"Have a seat in the parlor," Miss Nordstrom instructed. "I'll get us a snack. Would you like tea or hot chocolate?"

"Hot chocolate," the girls said in unison, then giggled.

Miss Nordstrom grinned, nodded, and went to the kitchen.

Even though Susan and Taylor had been in the parlor many times, they were still fascinated by the elegance of the decor. Everything appeared to be old and well maintained.

They sat down on an antique red, velvet couch and looked around.

"What's that smell?" Susan asked, wrinkling her nose.

Taylor sniffed. "I don't smell anything."

Susan looked down at the couch, frowning. She didn't find anything, so she looked at the small, round end table that sat beside her. It held a lamp and a shallow bowl with a mesh bag, which looked like it held potpourri.

Leaning closer, Susan sniffed. "Found it," she said, lifting the bag by the string and holding it out for Taylor to smell.

Taylor wrinkled her nose and gagged. "That reeks! Get it away from me!"

Susan made a disgusted face and put it back where she found it.

Miss Nordstrom entered the room at that exact moment, carrying a tray full of mugs of steaming beverages, small plates, forks, napkins, and pumpkin roll.

The girl's faces lit up as the pumpkin and spice aroma overpowered the stench of the little bag, but not before Miss Nordstrom saw their expressions.

"What's wrong?" she asked the girls, setting the tray down gently on the coffee table. "You look disgusted with something."

Taylor shrugged and looked at Susan.

"I was just sitting here and I smelled something funny," Susan said, picking up the little mesh bag to show Miss Nordstrom. "I found this. It *really* stinks."

Miss Nordstrom laughed. "If it bothers you, I'll put it some place else."

She took the bag from Susan, put it back in the bowl, and moved it to the top of an old piano that was in the opposite corner of the small room.

"Better?"

Susan smiled and nodded. "Yes, thanks. What was in it? Why do you keep something so smelly in here?"

"Susan," Taylor gasped, elbowing her friend in the side. "That was rude!"

Miss Nordstrom laughed. "Not at all, I have no problem answering those questions. The bag has a mixture of herbs in it. My great-grandma used to make those bags before every Halloween, to keep bad spirits out of the house. It's an old superstition. I can't say I really believe it, but doing it each year makes me feel closer to my family."

Both girls smiled politely and nodded. They knew Miss Nordstrom didn't have any living relatives, and didn't want to push the subject, taking what she said at face value.

They talked and laughed for the next ten minutes as they ate their delicious snack, forgetting about the stinking bag.

"Now," Miss Nordstrom said, putting her empty plate back on the tray. "What has brought you two to my doorstep this afternoon? You didn't look too happy when you arrived."

With the reminder of the reason for their visit, tears sprang to Susan's eyes, and she gushed out the whole tale of Tiger going missing while Taylor held her hand.

"Oh, that's terrible," Miss Nordstrom exclaimed. "No one's seen him? What does he look like?"

"He's a plump orange and yellow tiger-striped cat," Taylor said, as Susan was now crying too hard to speak. "He has a tie-dye collar with a little gold bell on it."

"Hmm, let me think," Miss Nordstrom said thoughtfully. "I don't recall seeing any strange cats around lately. Have you checked over by Mrs. Larson's? I've heard of all kinds of animals disappearing over there."

With the mention of Mrs. Larson, both girls froze, their faces going white with fear. Mrs. Larson was a crazy old lady that lived in an old rickety house on the hill. Her yard was always overgrown, and dark clouds and fog seemed to linger around the house. She was a witch, or so all the children believed.

"Mrs...Mrs...Larson?" Susan said in a quivery voice, swallowing hard. "You think she might have taken Tiger?"

Miss Nordstrom shrugged and sighed. "I'm not saying she did, but I've heard stories of her taking animals that she finds roaming around. If you don't find Tiger anywhere else, I would check there."

The girls glanced at each other; the knuckles of their clasped hands were now white from gripping so tightly. They were afraid of Mrs. Larson—always had been.

"I hate to rush you two out," Miss Nordstrom said, standing and picking up the tray now laden with empty plates and mugs. "I wasn't expecting company today, and I have an appointment soon. I wish you good luck in finding Tiger."

The girls mumbled their thanks for the refreshments and made polite good-byes, but as they walked out of the house, chills ran down their spines. They jumped as the door closed with a loud *thump* behind them. Thunder boomed from the sky where dark clouds had gathered. Lightning flashed and the wind picked up with a vengeance.

They glanced at Mrs. Larson's house on the hill, which was shrouded with dark storm clouds. The lightning flashed off the window, and made the house look like it was coming alive and wanted to eat them.

Thunder boomed again, and the girls screamed. They ran off the porch and all the way back to Susan's house, knowing it was about to storm. Just as they stepped through the door, closing it tightly behind them, rain poured from the fall sky, drowning the world in gray and stripping the radiant red, orange, and yellow leaves from the trees, laying them out in a murky carpet on the road and lawns.

The girls darted up the steps to Susan's room and talked in hushed voices about what they would do tomorrow—how they would find Tiger.

As a last resort, they would go to Mrs. Larson's, but only after they checked everywhere else.

* * *

The next morning was still overcast. Gray, damp clouds hung low to the ground, setting the perfect stage for Halloween. The girls met at the agreed upon time and continued their search. No one had seen Tiger.

"Let's just go do it," Taylor said. "The sooner we go and ask, the sooner we can get home and get ready to go trick-or-treating. Besides, I'm cold and hungry."

Susan nodded, her teeth chattering from cold and fear. "Okay."

Slowly the girls walked to the gate set in a high brick wall that surrounded Mrs. Larson's property. The land had been in her family for years, having been owned by the town's founder, who was Mrs. Larson's great-uncle.

They stood at the ornate wrought iron gate, staring at the twisted trees, overgrown bushes, and weed choked gravel driveway. Gulping, they pushed the gate open. It screeched in protest and a mass of black crows took flight from their hiding places in the trees. There were so many of them that the sky looked black with stars of gray where the clouds shown through.

"I don't want to do this," Susan whined. "Can't we just have my dad or someone come up here?"

"Your dad is at work, and it'll be dark by the time he gets home," Taylor said, trying to be brave. "Besides, if we don't do this now, we won't be back in time to trick-or-treat, and I don't want to miss that."

Susan nodded and took Taylor's hand in a death grip. They walked together, hand in hand, up the gravel drive to the house that stood on the top of the hill. The stones of the drive crunched under their feet with each step. Their eyes darted about anxiously, expecting some huge monster to come bounding out and gobble them up at any moment.

Before they knew it, they had made it to the house. It was an old Victorian made of red brick. Vines grew up the sides, like the fingers of vegetation were trying to grab the house and pull it down into the earth, swallowing it and the inhabitants forever.

Slowly, they stepped on the wooden steps that lead to the house; each one creaked ominously, causing their apprehension to grow. By the time they reached the top, they were both so tense that they moved in short, stilted steps toward the door.

The porch went all the way around the house, so after they knocked tentatively, with no answer, they decided to walk around the corner to see if there was a back door.

As they went around to the side porch, they saw a light. There was a large window close to the back corner of the house that was like the beacon of a light house to a stormy sea. The girls headed for it.

Kneeling down, they peeked over the windowsill to see what was inside. The room appeared to be a kitchen. Herbs hung from the ceiling on strings, small containers with hand written labels covered every available surface, and a large pot was steaming on the stove.

Mrs. Larson stepped into the room. Her gray and white hair stuck out from her head at odd angles. As she turned and took something out of a cabinet, they saw that she had attempted to tame her hair into a bun, but had failed. She wore a calico print dress that looked home-made and old—something that would have been worn twenty or thirty years ago. As she closed the cabinet, she turned to face the window.

The girls hurriedly ducked down, before slowly peeking in again.

They hadn't been seen.

They watched as Mrs. Larson stirred the contents of the pot, singing to herself. She walked over to a drawer and pulled it open, and that's when Susan saw it. Tiger's collar was hanging from the handle of the drawer!

With a gasp, Susan spun around to sit on her butt, facing away from the house. "She has him. She took Tiger. How are we supposed to get him back? For all we know, she's cooking him right now in that pot!"

"Shhh!" Taylor hissed. "Be quiet. We don't want to get caught; she'll probably cook and eat us, too!"

Just then, the window slid open and Mrs. Larson stuck her head out and looked down at them.

"Hi, girls," she said in a cracked voice. "Want to come in for something hot to drink?"

The girls screamed, jumped up, and ran. They were off the porch in moments, down the driveway in a minute, and as they passed through, they slammed the gate shut behind them. Only then did they stop to take a breath. Only then did they stop screaming.

They hurried to Taylor's house, where they were going to get ready to go trick-or-treating. They took turns taking showers, and then they had some soup to warm them up. It did the trick for their bodies, but their minds were still frozen in fear from their experience.

When they went back upstairs to get ready to go, Susan started to cry.

"I can't believe she ate him," she sobbed. "I loved him so much, and she ate him. It's just not fair."

Taylor hugged her friend. "I know. But there's nothing we can do about it now. We might as well try to have fun tonight. Maybe some time out with friends will make you feel better."

"I don't know," Susan sniffed. "I could tell my parents. They could call the police. Isn't that cruelty to animals or something?"

"We'd have to get evidence for that," Taylor said thoughtfully. "Maybe if we went back and got the collar, you know, as proof that she took him, then they could do something."

Susan shook her head, her eyes wide with fear. "I can't go back there. I'm too scared. She'll get us this time for sure!"

"Calm down, calm down," Taylor sighed and sat down on the bed. "We'll do it after we're done trick-or-treating. She should be asleep by then. All we have to do is find a way in and take the collar. I bet she doesn't even lock her doors. I mean, she's a witch, who would dare try to steal from her? They'd probably be cursed for life!"

Susan nodded, but still looked scared.

"Let's get our costumes on," Taylor said with a soft smile. "We don't want to be late for the candy!"

Susan laughed through her tears. "You know, we are getting kinda old for this. How many more years do you think we can get away with candy begging before they stop giving it to us?"

Taylor grinned. "I plan to try for a couple of years yet. After that, I'll just start throwing Halloween parties!"

For the next hour, the girls forgot about all their cares as they applied each other's make-up and dressed in their costumes. This year Susan was a giant teddy bear and Taylor was an undead fairy princess.

With pumpkin pails in hand, they left to beg for candy. The night flew by with friends they met along the way, and the excitement of seeing everyone's costumes.

Before they knew it, they were standing in front of the wrought iron gate, staring up at Mrs. Larson's house.

"I don't want to do this," Susan said.

"You want to report her for eating Tiger, don't you?" Taylor asked.

"Yes, but I don't want to go up there again."

"What are you two doing?" Miss Nordstrom asked, coming up behind them. She was dressed as a sexy rock star. "Trick-or-treating is almost over. The two of you shouldn't be out here all alone. Something bad might happen to you."

The girls looked at each other, wondering if they should tell Miss Nordstrom what was going on. They missed the malicious gleam in her eyes, and the slight smirk that fluttered across her face for an instant.

"Mrs. Larson took Susan's cat and ate him," Taylor said. "We saw his collar in her kitchen. Everything is true. She *is* a witch!"

"We have to go up there and get his collar," Susan gushed. "So we have proof when we tell the police."

"Oh, I see," Miss Nordstrom said. "Do you want me to come with you? You both look scared."

Taylor and Susan smiled with relief at having an adult come with them.

"That would be great," Taylor said.

Susan nodded in agreement—too choked up from relief to speak.

"I have to go and get something from my house first, okay?" Miss Nordstrom said. "You two wait right here."

In just minutes, Miss Nordstrom was back, carrying two strings with something attached to them.

"These are charm bags I had laying around the house," she explained. "My mom made them for us kids when we would go out on Halloween, to protect us from evil spirits. It's kind of like the bag you asked about yesterday, Susan. These are a little different, though."

She slid one over each girl's head, to dangle from their necks, over their costumes. They stunk worse than the bag in the parlor did.

"Where's yours?" Taylor asked, trying not to gag.

"I have one in my pocket," Miss Nordstrom said with a smile. "It's been in there all night."

"Oh, okay," Susan said, turning her head to try and breathe in some fresh air.

Together they stepped up to the gate. The two girls hung back a little, thinking about their earlier experience. Miss Nordstrom didn't have that problem, and she pushed it open. It screeched louder than it had earlier, and both girls shuddered.

Miss Nordstrom looked back over her shoulder. "You two coming?"

They nodded and followed her inside. The trees and the bushes were even more unnerving in the dark.

They hadn't gone very far when Susan started to yawn.

"I feel so weak and tired," she said, covering her mouth as she yawned yet again. "Do you mind if we take a break?"

Taylor was yawning, too. "A break does sound nice."

"I agree," Miss Nordstrom said with a gleeful smile. "Let's rest. I think I see a bench over there, just past that tree. Why don't you two go sit down?"

The girls nodded, and stumbling over to the bench, they sat down.

"Why do I feel so drowsy?" Susan mumbled as she almost fell asleep and would have fallen off the bench if Taylor hadn't been there to lean on.

Taylor kept dozing off herself, and would try to startle herself awake again, blinking like an owl and shaking her head.

Miss Nordstrom watched with amusement. "It's the charm bags I gave you. They'll put you to sleep and then I'll take you home. It's time for me to do my beauty spell again, and I'll be needing some parts of young girls for the potion. You two should do nicely. You're both young and subtle."

Susan finally fell asleep and landed in the overgrown grass with a *thump*.

Taylor whimpered, still trying to stay awake. "Why are you doing this to us? I thought you were our friend."

"I have no friends," Miss Nordstrom laughed. "I use people and I move on. I've been doing it for hundreds of years. Luckily my spells last for a long time, so I don't have to move too often."

"You're...you're a witch," Taylor gasped, before she too fell off the bench, sound sleep.

* * *

Susan woke up slowly. Her body was weak and it took an effort for her to move. She was surrounded by tall grass, and it was dark out. Her head throbbed with a headache. It was the strangest headache she ever had.

As she sat up, she looked around. There were trees, bushes, and a cement bench, but nothing else. Slowly, her mind started to work again, and she remembered where she was and what happened.

"Taylor?" she croaked, standing up. Dizziness overtook her and she immediately sat down on the bench.

After the world stopped spinning, she looked around again. Taylor was nowhere in sight, but she could now see a path of flattened grass that lead back to the driveway.

"Miss Nordstrom," she muttered to herself. "She must have taken her back to her house."

Standing again, Susan closed her eyes and willed the dizziness to go away. She needed to find help, and fast. Miss Nordstrom would be back for her soon, and she had to get away. But the closest person was Mrs. Larson. The thought of going to that house again still scared her. But the thought of being chopped up and cooked into some kind of potion scared her even more.

Stumbling and weaving, Susan made her way up the overgrown driveway. She tripped and fell over the weeds multiple times, and by the time she reached the house, her knees and her hands were scratched and bleeding.

She gulped hard before she lifted her foot and forced herself to climb the porch steps. She went to the door and knocked. No answer.

She stood there for a moment, thinking maybe she had just dreamed it all up, when she heard a rustling of leaves and a twig snap behind her. Turning, she saw Miss Nordstrom rushing up the driveway.

Susan pounded on the door with all her strength, yelling, "Help! Help!"

She glanced back to see Miss Nordstrom just entering the overgrown grass that surrounded the house. As she looked back, the door opened and she fell inside.

Mrs. Larson stood over her with her hands on her hips. She was wearing a long, white cotton night gown and her hair was even wilder than it had been before.

"Can I help you, dear?" Mrs. Larson asked, her voice cracking.

Susan lay speechless, looking outside at the now empty yard, and then up at Mrs. Larson.

"Can you talk? Cat got you tongue?"

At the mention of a cat, Susan's throat went dry and she feared she had made the biggest mistake ever coming here. The thought that Mrs. Larson and Miss Nordstrom were both witches and were working together hit her brain like a lightning bolt, making her gasp.

Susan began to tremble violently and tears slid down her cheeks. Closing her eyes, she lay back on the floor, thinking she was doomed. Something cold and wet touched Susan's ear, and then a rough tongue began licking her cheek. She opened her eyes to see Tiger!

Forgetting about the women she thought were trying to kill her, she sat up and squealed, picking up the cat to cuddle him close.

"Ah, so he belongs to you," Mrs. Larson said with a soft smile. "I found him yesterday, he'd hurt his paw and was laying on my porch."

Susan wiped the tears from her face and noticed that Tiger had a white bandage on his left hind leg. He wasn't eaten! He was rescued!

"I . . . I thought you ate him," Susan said softly.

"Oh no, dear. Why ever would you think that?"

"I thought you were a witch," Susan said, blushing and rubbing her now smiling face on Tiger's fur.

"That's just silly, dear," Mrs. Larson laughed. "I'm just an old woman that keeps to herself and takes care of injured animals when they come my way. There's no witches around here!"

Susan froze and looked up at Mrs. Larson, her eyes huge with fear. "Yes, there is. Miss Nordstrom is a witch. She tricked me and Taylor, that's my friend, to wear these charm bags, saying they would protect us. They put us to sleep and she planned to take us to her house and use our body parts to make a potion that would keep her looking young and beautiful! We have to save Taylor! She took her!"

"Calm down, dear," Mrs. Larson said. "I'm sure it was just a prank or something. Where's Taylor now?"

Susan stood up, still clutching Tiger. "It's not a prank! I'm telling the truth. We have to call the police. She has Taylor!"

"Okay, dear, okay," Mrs. Larson said. "We'll call the police, but I'm sure it's all a misunderstanding."

* * *

Dawn was just starting to light the distant horizon as Miss Nordstrom was lead out of her house in handcuffs.

"We've been looking for this one for a long time," one of the officers said to Taylor's dad. "She's been on the FBI's most wanted list for years. I, myself, have never believed in witches, but this has changed my mind."

Taylor was being loaded into the back of an ambulance to be checked out at the local hospital, although she seemed fine. They found her in Miss Nordstrom's basement, still asleep.

Upon investigating, they also found the charm pouch that Susan had been wearing, laying beside the stone bench. Luckily for her, it had gotten caught on a sharp corner where the cement had eroded and chipped, cutting the string that held it around her neck. Otherwise, she wouldn't have woken up, and they would never have caught Miss Nordstrom.

Mrs. Larson walked up to Susan, who was watching all the activity from across the street, wrapped in a fleece blanket. She put her arm around Susan and gave her a hug.

"You were very brave, dear. If it hadn't been for you, your friend would have died," she said.

Susan smiled at Mrs. Larson, still holding Tiger in her arms. "I'm glad you're a nice woman instead of a witch. It's strange that we had it all mixed up. The real witch pretended to be our friend, and you were just a nice woman we thought was strange. I'm sorry."

Mrs. Larson laughed. "Well, now you know that you can't believe what you hear about people. You just have to meet them and find out for yourself."

Susan giggled. "I guess so."

"Susan," her mother called as she walked across the street. "It's time to go home and get some rest. You've had a big night. I'll take you to visit Taylor at the hospital tomorrow."

"Okay, Mom," Susan said. "Can Mrs. Larson come, too? I'd love for Taylor to meet her. Oh, is that okay with you, Mrs. Larson?"

Both women laughed.

"That would be fine with me," Mom said.

"I'd love to, dear," Mrs. Larson smiled.

Susan and her mom started walking away when Susan handed Tiger to her mother, then ran back to Mrs. Larson and gave her a hug.

"Do you think I could come and visit you sometime, and you could teach me about taking care of hurt animals?"

Mrs. Larson laughed. "I'd like that very much."

* * *

Many years later, Susan was locking up her veterinary clinic to go home. She smiled, never tiring of seeing her name on the door. With a content sigh, she turned to walk down the street, heading home.

She pushed open the gate, and started up the well-maintained driveway. The crisp autumn air rustled the orange and red leaves that dangled from the pruned trees. Giggling, she caressed the bushes that were trimmed in the shapes of pumpkins, ghosts, and ghouls. Today was Halloween, and after dark, the children would come to her house to trick-or-treat. All the orange lights strung in the bushes would light the way to her house. The house on the top of the hill. The one she had bought off Mrs. Larson. The woman who had nurtured her passion for animals, and had been an inspiration to her life.

Standing at the bottom of the steps, Susan looked up at the house that had once scared her, which was now a place of warmth and friendship.

"Happy Halloween," she whispered, and went inside to put on her costume, knowing Taylor would be arriving soon to help her pass out candy.

RIP

THE GHOST OF OLD MAN HARRIS

KEVIN MILLIKIN

The ghost of old man Harris sat alone in the darkness, as he would always do. He was perched atop his open casket; he'd count the cracks in the floor, the ceiling and the wall. The old man would do just about anything to take his mind off the past and most importantly, the horrid racket just beyond his mausoleum.

In the coffin was an exquisite collection of the old man's skeletal remains. Before, the bones were white, as if someone had bleached the whole lot, but now a thinly veiled layer of dust blanketed the bones, the brick and the mortar. Hadn't old man Harris been a ghost, he might have gotten dusty as well.

Often times, the others would poke their heads in and comment on the mess he had turned the place into. As always, Harris would tell them to, "Go away," and return to his counting. Harris liked what the others deemed to be his *doom and gloom*; he felt it added character to his tomb.

The old man found no joy in being dead—not like the others. He couldn't understand why they felt the need to throw such festivities as though everyday was Halloween. For him, death was life's long overdue rest and now, given the time, that was all that he did.

The ghost of old man Harris wasn't like all the others. In fact, he despised them greatly, right down to the tiniest details of their own ghoulish existence. All of this was because Harris couldn't understand how on earth they could be having so much fun and be so dead.

He would watch them occasionally, when he knew they weren't looking. The old man would hide, cloaked within the shadows through the bars of his crypt. He didn't want them to know, more so, because he'd rather not give them an invitation to do the same to him.

He just couldn't imagine how all of the cemetery's residential ghouls, ghosts, monsters and the undead, would find so much fun living such an existence. Nightly, they would laugh and dance around the light of the funeral pyre. On occasion, when the excitement got too close to home, the old man's ghost would slink off his casket and scream, "You're dead, be quiet!" and "Go home!"

To which, often times they would reply, "Aw, but old man Harris, death is a grave, why would you dig it?"

"There's nothing fun about death," he would say. "And there was nothing fun about life either, now please, just go away!"

* * *

Truth be told, old man Harris wasn't always this way. Long before he had died; maybe fifty years or more, a younger Harris had served in the Second World War.

At the time, Harris was young, strong and fit. He knew right from wrong and always made sure to go out of his way to help others. Most importantly though, he was in love. In fact, he was madly in love with a beautiful young girl from Chicago named Mary who was a beautiful little thing, with soft blue eyes and curly blonde hair that seemed to radiate the sun's glow at all hours of the day. She was the embodiment of heaven on earth. Mary was an angel in a white dancing dress and black dancing shoes. Every weekend, the two of them would go out dancing at the ballrooms in town, where they'd dance until the first light of the morning.

"I love you," she told a younger, livelier Harris on the night before he was to be shipped out across the Atlantic, on the eve of his first war.

"I love you, too," he replied and he did, very much. In fact, he had planned to marry the girl upon his arrival back into the states, whenever that may be.

"Please be safe," she told him. Her words were heavy with genuine concern. "And please, don't be long," she begged as tears welled up behind her eyes.

It broke his heart knowing he could so easily break the young girl's heart. After all, Mary was the last girl he would ever want to hurt.

"I won't," he told her. "I'll be home before you know it." Even though Harris meant what he said, he was unaware that it would be just a little under four years before he would return back to America.

He arrived into New York City on July 9th, 1942. Making true to his promise, the first thing he set out to do after he stepped off the boat was to go out and get Mary the perfect ring so he could ask for her hand.

For four long years Harris spent abroad, and the couple wrote each other regularly, exchanging stories and all they had done, and most importantly, talking about their plans for the future. It was because of this that Harris decided it was the right time for the two of them to get married.

He spent his first day in New York City, far removed from all the attractions a tourist would do, and instead he wandered around, from jewelry store to jewelry store, pawn shop to department stores. He was looking for the perfect ring to give to the perfect girl.

Finally, he found it, a modest ring from a corner store pawn shop. Originally, he didn't plan on buying it, but when he first saw it, all he could do was picture his young love's face and that was all he needed.

With the ring in his pocket, he stepped back into the world, ready to travel back home and propose to Mary. He would too if he hadn't stepped off into the street, directly in front of an oncoming taxi cab.

When Harris awoke, he was home in a new strange land that the locals had deemed *Cemetery Drive*, and though large in scale, it paled in comparison to the colorful array sprung up across the underworld.

His first night there, a festive celebration was underway, a hazing of sorts for all the new arrivals. At first the ghost of Harris thought it was all for him, but it became apparent it was a nightly jubilee.

The fear he felt in no way compared to the anger he had for being taken away from his life and the perfect girl. He stood up on the hill, his ghost hovering above a headstone, and he looked outwards upon a sea of death. Skeletons and other inhuman oddities all looked back intently at him, their eyes and eyeless sockets locked and bemused, wondering what might unfold.

All Harris could muster was, "You all make me sick," before he turned and moved away, back to the crypt he had taken as his own.

* * *

"Harris, Mister Harris?"

He knew the voice before even turning around. It belonged to Shirley, a little dead girl of seven. She was pretty, with bulging blue eyes and a soft baby blue face. She had choked, that much was sure. Whenever she talked, she sounded as though she still had a mouthful of food.

The grumpy old ghost never knew how much the little girl liked him. At times, when he would leave for a walk in the morning's light, she would follow, asking him questions like, "What were you like in life? Were you always this grumpy? Why are you so grumpy?"

Harris didn't like the girl, even though she cared for him. He never knew what to say, so rather than the two of them walking the path, enjoying a simple conversation, he would simply say, "*Go away.*"

"What?" he finally asked, losing count of the cracks in the floor, he turned around to face the girl but she had never made eye contact.

"Um..." she repeated.

"What?" he snapped again, floating down from atop his casket. "Why are you bothering me? What's you're problem?"

She searched for the words in such a lighthearted way that only a child could do. "I've been asked to invite you out to the celebration tonight."

"No," he snapped, turning his head away.

"For a homecoming?" she persisted.

"Never." He had no interest in meeting his new neighbors, not when there were more cracks to count. The nerve these people had utterly bugged him. Just because you're dead doesn't give you an excuse to be so rude.

"But…"

"No."

"Please?"

"No."

"Why?"

"Well, I…" he muttered, settling back on the top of his casket. "I just don't want to. Yes, that's it. Just don't want to. It's as simple as that, and little girl, don't you know it's not polite to ask so many questions?"

She was silent. He tried counting the cracks again, but when he heard her sniffle, he lost all of his concentration. He tried counting again and again but lost it when the dead girl began to cry.

"Why do you care?" he asked, turning back to her.

She looked at him, her glossy eyes looking back, wide and saddened, and as if on cue, her lower lip began to quiver.

"Why do you care?" he repeated. "Why does it matter?"

"But what have we done?" Shirley inquired. "We've only tried to help you and all you do is treat us like dirt."

He thought about it and realized he had nothing to say, so instead he shook his head and remained silent. He let the little girl do the talking.

"We're sorry you've been dealt a bad hand, Mr. Harris, but what about the rest of us? I'm only nine. Do you think I wanted to die?"

All he could think was how bad he was at guessing people's age. He was off by two years.

"But we all have to put it behind us," she said. "And we try to make the best out of the worst. We've all lost and mourned. I'm sorry to bother you, but won't you please come out tonight? "

Again, he shook his head.

"Not even for Mary?" Shirley asked.

"What about Mary? Who told you about her?" he snapped. Inside, the old man's ghost felt strangely violated.

"Mary did," the little girl replied.

Harris was at a loss for words. "What?" he asked after a long pause. "She's here?"

Shirley looked at him as though she was studying him. She was a smart one, Harris realized, well beyond her age. It was at that moment that he realized he didn't mind the little girl so much. In fact, he enjoyed the conversation even if he didn't do much of the talking.

"Yes," she replied, almost reluctantly.

"Where?" he snapped, leaping forward, his ghostly hands grabbing the girl by her shoulders. His head was spinning with a thousand different thoughts a second. His heart pounded, fearful and excited all in the same moment.

"Tonight," she said, "I'll come back tonight for you."

With that, the ghost of the little girl turned and left. Floating back down the path in which she came. She had left the old man alone with his thoughts. His mind racing with the: who, what, when and where's.

Harris paced around the crypt, all the while thinking of his long lost love. In fact, it was the first in a very long time that he had thought of anything except himself, and while he didn't know about it at the time, he felt a strange *tick* in the back of his mind that something new was on the rise.

As the hours passed, the sun fell behind the land, giving birth to a bad moon rising, bringing with it the festivities and excitement that such homecoming celebrations provided. *Samhain* and *Dia de los Muertos* couldn't hold a candle to the nightly parties held within the gates of Cemetery Drive.

The night was full of fun and games, all of which was unseen by mortal eyes and yet, it was a *private* party that everyone was *dying* to get into.

That night, Harris stood motionless by the mausoleum gates. Off in the horizon burned an orange glow as every ghoul, ghost and spook began to light their fires. Watching them only seemed to intensify the throbbing within his heart; it pained him to know that his Mary was out there somewhere, possibly waiting for him.

He thought about slipping out between the bars and finding her himself; taking her by the arm, kissing her and telling her just how much he had missed her and how he had always felt. He wondered if she knew he was going to propose.

The gripping fear fumbling in his belly kept him stationary, so instead he waited for Shirley's return, and eventually, she did come. Upon seeing his hopeless stare, she shook her soft baby blue locks and groaned, "Come on."

And he did, slipping out between the gates. The old man took the girl's hand, and they began their stroll down the walkway, but after a few seconds, Harris all but stopped.

"What is it?" Shirley croaked, more than a little annoyed that the older specter had stopped.

"Nothing," he whispered, looking at their conjoined hands, more or less amazed that he had taken her hand without a second thought.

"Well, come on then, please. This isn't the only thing I have to do tonight, Mr. Harris."

He nodded, taking a second to get back on the mental horse. He wondered how long the little girl had been dead since she was so smart.

Together they went, making their way down the cobblestone walkway. Past the werewolves, the goblins and a couple of zombies who had stopped to catch a bite to eat. They all stopped what they were doing when the ghost of old man Harris and Shirley walked by. It made him nervous to see all those eyes looking back on him, but he shook it off. He had never cared what others thought of him, and as he floated on past, he vowed not to start now.

Time passed at a crawl, his nervousness never ceasing. They kept down the walkway for what seemed to be forever and ever. The path they followed went forward and backwards, following the curves and the bends. It seemed to Harris that the underworld was a never-ending land, and no matter where he seemed to look, there were new places and new faces to see.

"There," she said, squeezing his hand. She pointed forward, down a crooked pathway that branched off the one they followed. He strained his eyes, and looking upward beyond the crooked and dilapidated headstones, he saw her.

Mary sat there, her hair softly blowing in the windless air. The night shown greatly through her spiritual body, and her back was turned to him.

"Mary!" he cried out as he let go of Shirley's hand. He did all that he could to make her aware of him, but his nerves crippled him, reducing his cries into a barely audible whimper.

He moved forward up the hill, but his ghostly legs could only take him as fast as the wind on this still night.

"Mary!" he cried again, gaining his voice.

He stopped as the vision of Mary on the hill cocked her head slightly as though she heard him. Did she hear him? It only pushed Harris further.

"Mary," he cried, "it's me, Harris!"

There was no mistaking it, she had heard him. Mary turned her head in the direction of his voice, and though she was distant, he could have sworn he could see the beauty of her face.

He looked back, hoping that he could catch a word or two of encouragement from Shirley, but the girl was gone. He sighed, knowing it was now or never. He pushed forward, continuing up the hill.

"Harris?" Mary asked as she floated down from her headstone. "Harris, is that really you?"

"Yes, it's me," he smiled. It was an odd feeling. He hadn't broke a smile in years, maybe more. He never thought twice about it but now, with this new turn of events, it had come easily as though it was second nature.

"I've waited so long for this," she said.

"Me too," he told her.

She was older now and even more beautiful than he remembered. She smiled as they embraced. Harris went limp in her arms. All of the comfort he had lost over the years returned with such vigor, that he felt no need to fight it. It was rather like a wave he could ride, and wherever it would take him was fine, as long as she was there.

Together, they walked hand in hand. Most of the time, they remained silent, intimidated by the presence of the other. But when they did talk, it was nothing less than heavenly.

After Harris had died, Mary had remained alone, mourning the loss of her one great love. Her entire life through, she never married and never loved, fearing that if she did, she would never have the opportunity to see him again. She had lived her life as a teacher before retiring at the gentle age of eighty-two.

"You're beautiful," he told her as she finished telling him her life's story.

"No, oh, no," she modestly giggled, blushing as she did. "I'm an old lady now, not the same girl I was when you left."

Harris smiled, looking into her light blue eyes.

"What?" she asked when he failed to reply.

"Yes you are," he smiled. "You're just as beautiful as the day I first met you."

She smiled as he took her hand and together they walked along the shores of the nearby lake.

"Don't ever leave me again," she told him.

"I won't," he replied as he squeezed her hand. Everything had come full circle for the old ghost named Harris. For now he was back together with the girl he thought he would never see again, and the love he thought he had all but lost was with him forever. "I promise."

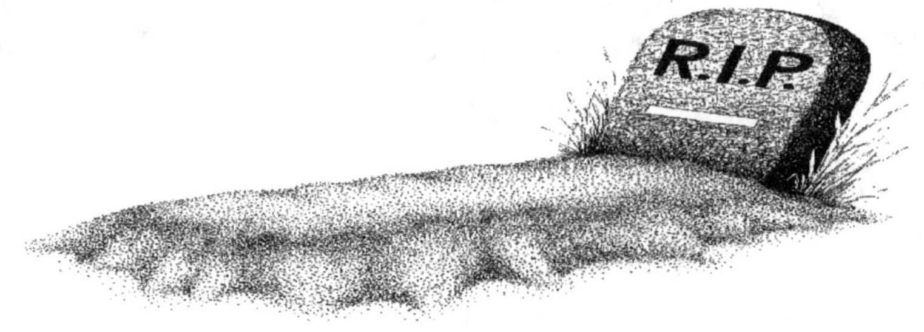

SUGAR-FUELED NIGHTMARE

GARY McKENZIE

"**M**om! I'm home!" Kenny yelled as he slammed the door behind him. He threw his bag of candy on the table, knocking the freshly-carved pumpkin off of it.

"What was that?" his mother yelled from the living room.

"Nothing!" he answered a little too quickly.

He fluidly removed his Circus Clown Halloween costume, and without an ounce of guilt, tossed it over the splattered remains of the pumpkin. He then grabbed his bag of candy, ran to his bedroom, and scattered his colorful, sugar-filled treasure on the floor.

Candy of all shapes and sizes tantalized the six year-olds taste buds.

"Eat me first!" they all seemed to call out simultaneously.

Just as he reached for his favorite chocolate and peanut butter morsel, his mother called out.

"Kenny!" she called. "Take your bath and get to sleep. You have school in the morning!"

"Aw, Mom!" Kenny whined. "Can't I have some candy first?"

"No!" she yelled back. "Bath, then bed. Candy tomorrow!"

With a huff, Kenny grabbed his pajamas and a fistful of candy and stomped to the bathroom. He turned the bathtub's nozzle on high so that his mother would hear the running water. This served to hide the crinkling of wrappers as the naughty child opened and quickly consumed his precious candy. He washed his face, only for the purposes of removing the white make-up, but still forgot to wash behind his ears; leaving smudges of white paint. After five minutes—the time it took to polish off his handful of sweets—he turned off the water, put his hands into it and rubbed his wet hands through his hair, giving the illusion that he had actually showered.

With a gob of chocolate still smeared across his lips, he walked into the living room to say 'good night' to his mother. As usual, she was passed out in front of a blaring television, wrapped in a robe with rollers in her hair and a lit cigarette that had dwindled down to mostly ash, which now dangled dangerously from her cracked lips.

With a shrug of his shoulders, he walked to his bedroom, grabbed some more candy, and crawled into bed. Tossing and turning, he eventually ended up staring at the ceiling until his sugar-rush dissipated and he fell asleep.

When Kenny opened his eyes, he found himself in a strange, new world. Weirder yet was that he was now wearing a cowboy outfit. He sat in a field of pink and yellow Easter-basket grass beneath a starless, midnight blue sky. Not far from him was a path dimly lit by orange, yellow and white candy-corns. He stood up and made his way across the plastic grass. His movements created a disturbing cross between a whisper and a hush as the pastel-colored plain crinkled underneath his feet.

He made his way to a gravelly, winding path which smelled like Ovaltine. He followed it to a large house which loomed over the landscape from out of a children's board game.

As he neared the dirty white building, strange glowing stones started to rise from the now green, plastic grass which surrounded the path. Curiosity set in and Kenny decided to leave the safety of the candy corn light and approached one of the newly risen, stained-glass-looking cubes.

On the front of the hard-candy block were the words, ***R.I.P. Kenny, 2004-2010***.

Mesmerized by the cryptic writing, Kenny didn't notice that he was next to an open grave until a white-chocolate covered hand reached out and grabbed his ankle.

"Trick-or-treat," groaned the skeleton as it continued to make its way out of the cold, dark pit.

Kenny jerked back his leg and escaped the vice-like grip of the skeleton, only to fall back into the grasp of another, who had started to emerge from the open grave behind him.

"Smell my feet," it growled as it yanked Kenny's other ankle.

"Give me something good to eat," the two skeletons sang in unison.

Kenny struggled backwards and escaped from the second skeleton's grasp only to stumble back into the waiting arms of the first skeleton, which was now fully emerged from its grave.

"... Like your brains!" it loudly whispered into the frightened boy's ear. Its breath reeked of spoiled milk.

Kenny squirmed like an eel in a vat of Vaseline. Through sheer fear and determination, the child managed to free himself and made a break for the path.

The second skeleton jumped in Kenny's way. Taking a lesson from Little League, Kenny dropped to the ground and slid for home plate—right between the stalking creature's boney legs. Once behind the fleshless fiend, he kicked the skeleton, and sent it crashing into the first one. With a rattling sound vaguely similar to dominos falling, the skeletons crashed to the ground and shattered into a hundred tiny fragments.

Back on the candy corn path, Kenny ran to the towering mausoleum. He scurried up the front steps, raised his fist to pound on the door, and stopped. His eyes grew in disbelief as the door slowly creaked open on its own accord. He shook his head, not caring about who lived there, and more concerned about getting away from the skeletons than what was inside, he pushed into a brightly lit, sterile room and slammed the door closed. With his back against the door, he let himself slide down to the floor and took a moment to catch his breath.

"Hello?" he called out only to hear it echo back. "Hello? Anybody here?"

After a few uncomfortable seconds, there was a whisper.

"Kenny," it said. "Come here, Kenny."

Immediately, goose bumps covered the young boy's body. Much to his own surprise, he found himself walking down the long corridor toward a flickering green light. It was as if he had no control over his actions.

"What am I doing?" he asked himself. "I don't want to go over there. I just want to go home."

Before he knew it, he was turning the corner and facing toward the source of the glowing green light. In front of him sat a scarecrow in a chair made out of human bones. One of its thin legs was casually draped over an armrest. On top of its shoulders sat a large pumpkin with angry eyes and a wicked smile carved into it. From inside its hollow head was a black candle with an eerie, green flame.

"I've been waiting for you," it said.

Kenny wanted to turn and run but he couldn't. He was frozen with fear.

The scarecrow held out one of its straw hands and showed Kenny what looked like a white coin with a red spiral on it. With a careful movement, the scarecrow's wrist began to rotate round and round.

Staring at the hypnotic piece of peppermint candy, Kenny's eyelids began to feel heavy. His primal urge to flee had all but disappeared.

"For years," the scarecrow began, "you and your family have been intentionally slaughtering my spawn. What makes it worse is that you do it all in the name of fun, not necessity."

"What are you talking about?" Kenny asked as he struggled to snap out of his hypnotic trance. "We've never killed anyone!" Before he could say anything else, he felt a shifting weight in his right hand. He looked down only to see that he was holding a grayish-orange, rotted pumpkin. The decaying vegetable slowly looked up at him.

"Murderer," it whispered through its withered mouth. Once pointed teeth now limply folded into the sunken cavity that had been its face. Suddenly, thousands of flies poured from its mouth and eye sockets and swarmed over the boy; breaking his trance.

Kenny dropped the decaying head. It splattered across the floor with a thunderous shriek of a thousand lost souls.

"Is it funny to carve open our heads and scoop out my helpless children?" the scarecrow asked. "Let's see how you like it!"

The creature reached for the boy. Its arms of straw and vine started to stretch far beyond their normal length, inching closer and closer to the frightened child. A maniacal laugh filled the room.

A surge of adrenaline rushed through Kenny's body. He was finally able to move of his own free will. Just as the creeping hands were about to grab him, he turned around and broke for the entrance.

The scarecrow's hands continued to reach for the boy. With a desperate swipe, the razor sharp claws of straw scraped the back of the cowboy vest, shredding it.

Turning the corner, Kenny noticed that the once empty hallway to the entrance was now lined with zombified clowns, standing motionless against the wall. Flakes of skin—or was it merely paint—fell off their faces and silently floated to the ground. They reminded him of suits of armor in an old castle.

Not wanting to get caught by the still growing arms of the psychotic scarecrow, he sprinted toward the now open and inviting door. As he neared the first clown, tiny bells from its colorful hat jingled as it tipped its head back. A pink rectangle began to jut out from a bloody slit in the clown's throat. Just as he passed the peculiar harlequin, the pink piece of candy shot out at the boy.

Instinctively, Kenny ducked and watched as the strange brick crashed into the opposite wall. Hitting the spotless floor, the mysterious morsel sprouted four pipe-cleaner legs and started running after the child. The rapid clicking of its tiny feet hitting the tile sent chills up Kenny's spine.

Running faster than he had ever run before, Kenny broke for the door. As he feared, each of the seven remaining clowns launched a killer Pez-like creature at him. The clacking of tiny feet on tile echoed through the hallway, almost to the point of becoming deafening, but Kenny was determined to escape.

As he neared the exit, he could feel the breeze from the outside world and smell the spearmint in the air. With a mighty lunge, the boy dove, head first, toward the doorway, hit the slick linoleum floor and slid out of the House of Horrors. Once his feet crossed over the threshold, the giant oak door behind him slammed shut all by itself.

Leaning over, hands on his knees to catch his breath, Kenny noticed that during his stay in the mausoleum, the sky had changed from midnight blue to an apocalyptical maroon. His costume had also changed from that of a cowboy into that of a caped superhero. In between his heavy breaths, he heard a familiar tune playing from nowhere in particular.

"It sounds like the ice cream truck," Kenny mumbled. "Only slower and creepier."

The candy corn path which once led the way to the mausoleum was no longer there. Instead, it had been replaced by giant lollipops. Colorful, colossal orbs balanced on top of thin white sticks. Inside each towering lollipop was a child frantically banging on the semi-transparent, candy wall. Muffled screams of 'Help me!', 'Let me out!', and "I want my Mommy!' went unanswered.

There was a bone-chilling scream from behind the awed child. Kenny quickly turned around and noticed three white ghosts made of marshmallow floating toward him. Their chocolate-drop eyes started to melt and their moans grew louder.

"This is crazy!" the frightened boy screamed and sprinted away from the floating apparitions.

Crossing the ever-changing landscape, he came across a forest of Weeping Willowish trees which loomed all around. From their lifeless branches hung long, thin, red and black licorice vines, which swayed gently in the breeze.

Feeling that he was safe enough to catch his breath, Kenny sat beneath one of the trees and began to cry.

"What's going on?" he wondered to himself in-between sniffles.

Too busy rubbing at his tear-filled eyes, he didn't notice one of the red vines silently slithering toward him until it was too late. The wormlike piece of candy quickly wrapped itself around the boy's leg and began to tighten.

"No!" Kenny yelled as he struggled to free himself. He noticed that other strands of licorice were quickly approaching. High above the child, a black strand silently started to fashion itself into noose.

In the back of his mind, a tiny part of his subconscious reminded him that these creatures were merely candy. Leaning over, he grabbed the red vine that was pulling at his leg and sunk his teeth into the edible rope.

The injured licorice strand became lifeless and fell from around his leg. He frantically untangled himself before any of the other licorice ropes could ensnare him and cautiously backed away.

Luckily, he caught a glimpse of a black noose coming at him from out of the side of his vision. With a duck and roll maneuver he learned from one of his video games, he managed to escape a long, drawn out death.

Hoping that the end of the forest was nearby, he ran blindly away from the killer trees.

Finally having some luck on his side, he cleared out of the shadowy forest and came upon a flowing, crystal blue river. Looking to the left and to the right, he saw that there was nowhere to cross. His choices were limited to either going back into the forest or swimming across.

Before he could make a decision, the ground began to shake and a loud, thundering noise steadily approached. Looking over the treetops, Kenny watched a giant green Gummy Bear rip one of the licorice Weeping Willows out of the ground. The red and black strands tried desperately to strangle the giant creature, but the entire plant was tossed over the bear's shoulder without a second thought.

Kenny stood on the river's edge, dumbfounded. The green bear noticed the boy and licked its snout in anticipation of devouring the frightened morsel. As a giant green paw reached for him, Kenny turned and dove into the water. He swam as fast as he could. Halfway across the river, he glanced back and saw that the Gummy Bear was wading into the water.

A humongous wave smacked Kenny in the face, temporarily blinding him and causing him to choke on the sweet water. Violently coughing and spitting flavorful liquid out of his mouth, he noticed that something was wrong.

He blinked his eyes rapidly until the droplets of water dissipated, allowing him to focus more clearly. He saw the giant bear madly thrashing as little red fish dove at the gummy flesh. Looking down into the surrounding water, he noticed that the little red fish had shiny, razor sharp, silver teeth.

Within seconds, the gelatinous creature had lost one of its legs and toppled into the water. A massive wave rushed toward Kenny and carried him all the way to the other side of the river.

Breathlessly, he crawled onto dry land. He looked back just in time to see the giant Gummy Bear's head disappear into a frothy sea of foam caused by the starving Swedish-Piranhas.

"No more," Kenny said to himself as he tightly shut his eyes and wished for it to be all over. "No more. No more. I just want to go home." With the tiniest glimmer of hope, he peeked out one eye.

In front of him sprawled another forest of trees; only these looked even creepier than the last ones. All of the new trees were black and twisted, kind of like an olive tree that had survived a forest fire. None of the brittle branches showed any signs of life, and yet there were hundreds of rotted, brown apples lying on the ground. Neon yellow worms, the size of small snakes, slithered in and out of the spoiled fruit.

Frequently stepping over the decayed apples, Kenny found himself deep in the forest. He approached one of the strange looking trees. There was something unusual about the knothole in the center of the trunk. Bending closer to the wooden oddity, he slowly reached out and poked the knothole, dead center. The gnarled wood split open, revealing an eye.

The tree branches started shaking violently. Soon, the entire forest of mutant trees had their single eye open and were staring at the young intruder. The angry rustling of their branches soon reached a deafening level. Just as quickly as it began, it stopped; leaving an uncomfortable silence.

Feeling paranoid, Kenny quickly turned in circles, not knowing what to expect or where to expect it to come from.

From above, a hint of bright red caught the corner of his vision. Tilting his head up, yet still careful to keep an eye out for any sudden movement, he noticed that the red coloring came from a fresh apple which hung from an unnaturally barren branch. Then he saw another, and another. The radiant fruit was sprouting like large red water-balloons and growing to immense proportions right before his eyes.

With long, thin branches that resembled a witch's fingers, one of the trees twisted until it clasped an apple. With another flash of movement, it threw the apple at the unsuspecting child.

Having always been a great dodgeball player, Kenny snapped out of his daze and dove to the ground a split second before the apple hit him. The red missile crashed to the dirt beyond him and exploded into shrapnel of razorblades.

Much to Kenny's horror, the other trees started to follow suit and threw their fruit of death at him. Never before had he leapt, dodged, ducked and rolled away from so many obstacles.

For a moment, he felt as if he was possessed by his favorite superhero. Razors whizzed past his ears with a deadly hiss. Every so often, he would feel a tear at his shirt, pants and skin. Glancing down, he noticed blossoms of bright red blood beginning to soak into his shredded costume.

He soon spotted a shimmer of light in front of him. He put down his head and sprinted toward it; zigging and zagging like a drunken madman just so he would stay out of the crosshairs of the bomb-throwing trees.

Glancing up, he noticed that the glow was coming from a calm river. An apple-bomb exploded behind him, sending a razorblade slicing across his earlobe. With hot blood flowing down his neck, he dove into the golden tranquility.

There was no splash. It was more of a *plop*.

"It's not water!" Kenny yelled in disbelief. "It's honey! I'm stuck!"

Struggling against the sticky substance, he frantically twisted and turned while he searched for something to grab on to. He saw a puff of wool-looking material dangling above him. With great effort, using muscles he didn't even know he had, he managed to free one of his arms from the golden goop.

Stretching to what seemed impossible lengths, Kenny snagged the cottony branch. For what seemed like forever, he finally freed his other arm and started to climb, hand over hand, out of the honey. Higher and higher he went as strands of honey stretched and snapped. The hungry bog managed to snag one souvenir from the child's visit; his shoe.

Wrapping his still sticky arm around the fluffy white branch, Kenny looked down and watched his shoe slowly disappear into the golden honey.

"Mom's gonna kill me," he thought to himself as he wiggled his toes.

Taking some time to catch his breath, Kenny surveyed his surroundings. All around were white, pink, and baby blue puffs of cotton. He looked down, it seemed much further than he had actually climbed, and noticed that the tree trunks were large cones of white paper. The intense aroma of spun sugar wafted into his nostrils.

"Cotton candy!" he exclaimed. He bent close to a fluffy mass and proceeded to lick it. "Mmm," he mumbled and bit into the nearest branch. The delicate concoction gently adhered to his face.

But something was wrong.

He couldn't breathe!

He grabbed the sugary mesh that was stuck to his face and frantically struggled to pull the sticky substance off.

As he thrashed around, he lost his balance on the tree limb and fell. Instead of hard ground breaking his bones, he landed softly in a netting of finely spun cotton candy. It cradled him like a loving bedspread.

Looking around, Kenny guessed he was close enough to the ground so that he could just jump off and continue to look for a way out of the weird world he was in. The only problem was that he couldn't move. The cotton candy clung to him even stronger than before. With each struggling movement, he managed to tangle himself in the webbing worse than before. He soon found himself immobile. That's when the web began to vibrate.

Directly above him, eight red eyes stared at him from the shadows. As the web shook even more violently, the silhouette of a spider, wearing a top hat, came into view. The hairy arachnid opened its mandibles and smiled at its prey. Long strands of poisonous saliva slowly dripped from its mouth. Closer and closer, the predator inched towards the helpless boy.

He felt his heart beating harder than it ever had before. He could almost feel his chest preparing to explode from the inside. With a desperate inhale of air, he screamed for his life. "*Noooooo!*"

Kenny quickly sat up in his darkened bedroom. Hair was plastered to his head with cold sweat. His pajama bottoms were also wet; but not from perspiration. Catching his breath, he frantically turned his head left and right to make sure he was back in the safety of his room. A cool breeze from an open window caused the curtain to billow.

From the crack underneath his closed door, he spotted a light which had just flicked on. Slow, shuffling feet from the living room approached his door.

Without warning, the door exploded inwards, violently slamming into the wall with a thunderous bang. Shadowed in the doorway was the pumpkin-headed scarecrow, the severed head of Kenny's mother dangling from its hand of straw and vines. Her eyes had been scooped out and a lit candle shone deeply from inside her mouth.

The scarecrow's carved mouth turned upwards into a cruel, wicked, smile.

"Trick-or-treat, Kenny!"

ABOUT THE WRITERS

Terry Alexander lives on a small farm near Porum, Oklahoma with his wife Phyllis. Together they have three children and nine grandchildren. They both enjoy sitting back with a good book on a rainy afternoon. His work has been published in Memories and Make Believe, Writing on Walls III, Echoes of the Ozarks V, Frontier tales.com and Night of the Wolf and End of Days III for Living Dead Press. Contact Terry at terryale@crosstel.net. He is a member of the Oklahoma Writers Federation, Ozark Writers League and the Arkansas ridge Writers.

Rebecca Besser lives in Ohio with her husband and little man. She's a graduate of the Institute of Children's Literature, a member of Write-On Writers and the Ohio Poetry Association (OPA). Her writing has appeared in the Coshocton Tribune, Irish Story Playhouse, Spaceports & Spidersilk, joyful!, Soft Whispers, Illuminata, Common Threads, and Golden Visions Magazine. She also has stories published in multiple anthologies by Living Dead Press, where she is currently an editor.
Visit her website to learn more about her: www.rebeccabesser.com

Mark Christopher is employed as an industrial hygienist by day and a horror writer by night. His passion for the macabre left him dissatisfied with many of the zombie stories and movies shambling around, so he was determined to blaze a new trail - one littered with slick patches of gore and more than a few empty shotgun shells.. He is the author of "Faye Believes," "Riser," "The Wanderer," and "The Glass Coffin. He's a graduate of Louisiana State University and currently resides in Baton Rouge, Louisiana.

Mariah Deitrick is a graduate from the Institute of Children's literature, and has had several short stories published for all ages. She currently lives in Iowa with her husband and four children where she enjoys fighting off zombies, monsters, or any other creature that tries invading her home.

Frank Collia is a writer and librarian living in Tampa, FL. He has been published in two previous Living Dead Press anthologies

David French lives in Virginia, and has a great love of classic horror movies. They inspire him to write the fun and frightening stories he hopes others will enjoy.

Anthony Giangregorio is the author and editor of more than 45 novels and anthologies, almost all of them about zombies.
His work has appeared in Dead Science by Coscomentertainment, Dead Worlds: Undead Stories Volumes 1-7, and Wolves of War by Library of the

Living Dead Press. He also has stories in End of Days: An Apocalyptic Anthology Vol. 1-4, the Book of the Dead series Vol. 1-5 by LDP, Zombie Zoology by Severed Press, and two anthologies with Pill Hill Press.

He is also the creator of the popular action/zombie series titled Deadwater and his action/ horror novel Dead Rage is being optioned for a movie.

Check out his website at www.undeadpress.com.

Dane T. Hatchell lives in Baton Rouge Louisiana. In his youth he was a fan of old school horror movies, and a collector of magazines such as Creepy and Eerie. Published stories in various anthologies include: Dead Worlds 6, The Book of Horror, Night of the Wolf, and End of Days 3 & 4. You can contact Dane at Enadious@gmail.com. Special thanks to Sarah Graves for her contributions as my copy editor.

Gary McKenzie lives in Chicago, IL and is the author of the Gingerbread Kingdom books. His first published horror stories can be found at www.houseofhorror.org/uk issue 9 (Shoebox Funeral) and lucky issue 13 (The Pocket Giant).

Kevin Millikin lives in Portland, Oregon though he was born and raised in Northern California. His previous story, "Scent of Rot" appeared in the Living Dead Press anthology Dead Worlds: Volume 6. He is also currently working on a number of projects that will be making their appearances later this year. When he's not writing he spends all of his time with his girlfriend, Cristin and their two psychotic kittens: Gus-Gus and Cobbler. He can be reached at: www.facebook.com/kevin.millikin

David Renfrow is a fiction writer who lives just outside of York, PA with his wife Stacy and their dog Jasmine. He writes mainly in the genres of horror, dark fantasy, and science fiction. David attends Messiah College, where he is a senior in their creative writing program. David's work has appeared in the horror magazine Dark Gothic Resurrected, as well as several anthologies from both Living Dead Press and Pill Hill Press.

David can be reached at zombiedave09@gmail.com

Hope Yandell is eleven years old and a National Merit Scholar. She has won the Nicholas Green Award this year for leadership, mathematics and community service. She has also been invited to a junior scholar's banquet in Washington D.C. this summer in recognition of her academic success. Hope has won several local short story and poetry contests. Her Red Ribbon artwork won first place in the statewide competition in Oklahoma. She and her parents have just completed a soft horror, short story anthology entitled Dream Weavers.

PLAYING GOD: A ZOMBIE NOVEL
by Jeffery Dye

It was supposed to be a regeneration virus to help soldiers on the battle-field—regrowing limbs and healing wounds— but a simple act of carelessness unleashed it on an unsuspecting world.

For the virus was not perfected, and once exposed, the host quickly dies, only to rise again as one of the undead.

As countries are quickly overrun, scientists and military teams battle to contain the outbreak.

There is no other option.

If the infection continues to spread, soon the entire globe will be consumed. And perhaps that will be a just punishment for a mankind that dared to try to play God.

DEAD HOUSE: A ZOMBIE GHOST STORY
by Keith Adam Luethke

The old mansion on the edge of town, aptly named Dead House, has a history of blood, pain, and death, but what Victor Leeds knows of this past only scratches the surface of the true horrors within.

But when his girlfriend is attacked by a shadowy figure one rainy night, he soon finds himself caught up in a world where the dead walk and ghostly wraiths abound. And to make matters worse, a pair of serial killers are fulfilling carefully made plans, and when they are done, the small town of Stormville, New York will run red. The last ingredient to open the gates of Hell, and plunge this small upstate town into madness, is rain.   And in Stormville, it pours by the gallons.

The Lazarus Culture
by Pasquale J. Morrone

Secret Service Agent Christopher Kearns had no idea what he was up against. Assigned on a temporary basis to the Center for Disease Control, he only knew that somehow it was connected to the lives of those the agency pro-tected...namely, the President of the United States. If there were possible terrorist activities in the making, he could only guess it was at a red alert basis.

When Kearns meets and befriends Doctor Marlene Peterson of the Breezy Point Medical Center in Maryland, he soon finds that science fiction can indeed become a reality. In a solitary room walked a man with no vital signs: dead. The explanation he received came from Doctor Lee Fret, a man assigned to the case from the CDC. Something was attached to the brain stem. Something alive that was quickly spreading rapidly through Maryland and other states.

Kearns and his ragtag army of agents and medical personnel soon find them-selves in a world of meaningless slaughter and mayhem. The armies of the walking dead were far more than mere zombies. Some began to change into whatever it was they ate. The government had found a way to reanimate the dead by implanting a parasite found on the tongue of the Red Snapper to the human brain. It looked good on paper, but it was a project straight from Hell.

The dead now walked, but it wasn't a mystery. It was The Lazarus Culture.

DEAD RAGE
by Anthony Giangregorio
Book 2 in the Rage virus series!

An unknown virus spreads across the globe, turning ordinary people into bloodthirsty, ravenous killers.

Only a small percentage of the population is immune and soon become prey to the infected.

Amongst the infected comes a man, stricken by the virus, yet still retaining his grasp on reality. His need to destroy the *normals* becomes an obsession and he raises an army of killers to seek out and kill all who aren't *changed* like himself. A few survivors gather together on the outskirts of Chicago and find themselves running for their lives as the specter of death looms over all.

The Dead Rage virus will find you, no matter where you hide.

CHRISTMAS IS DEAD: A ZOMBIE ANTHOLOGY
Edited by Anthony Giangregorio

Twas the night before Christmas and all through the house, not a creature was stirring, not even a. . . zombie?

That's right; this anthology explores what would happen at Christmas time if there was a full blown zombie outbreak. Reanimated turkeys, zombie Santas, and demon reindeers that turn people into flesh-eating ghouls are just some of the tales you will find in this merry undead book. So curl up under the Christmas tree with a cup of hot chocolate, and as the fireplace crackles with warmth, get ready to have your heart filled with holiday cheer. But of course, then it will be ripped from your heaving chest and fed upon by blood-thirsty elves with a craving for human flesh! For you see, Christmas is Dead!

And you will never look at the holiday season the same way again.

BLOOD RAGE
(The Prequel to DEAD RAGE)
by Anthony Giangregorio

The madness descended before anyone knew what was happening. Perfectly normal people suddenly became rage-fueled killers, tearing and slicing their way across the city. Within hours, Chicago was a battlefield, the dead strewn in the streets like trash.

Stacy, Chad and a few others are just a few of the immune, unaffected by the virus but not to the violence surrounding them. The *changed* are ravenous, sweeping across Chicago and perhaps the world, destroying any *normals* they come across. Fire, slaughter, and blood rule the land, and the few survivors are now an endangered species.

This is the story of the first days of the Dead Rage virus and the brave souls who struggle to live just one more day.

When the smoke clears, and the *changed* have maimed and killed all who stand in their way, only the strong will remain.   The rest will be left to rot in the sun.

DEAD END: A ZOMBIE NOVEL
by Anthony Giangregorio
THE DEAD WALK!

Newspapers everywhere proclaim the dead have returned to feast on the living!

A small group of survivors hole up in a cellar, afraid to brave the masses of animated corpses, but when food runs out, they have no choice but to venture out into a world gone mad.

What they will discover, however, is that the fall of civilization has brought out the worst in their fellow man.

Cannibals, psychotic preachers and rapists are just some of the atrocities they must face.

In a world turned upside down, it is life that has hit a Dead End.

DEADFREEZE
by Anthony Giangregorio
THIS IS WHAT HELL WOULD BE LIKE IF IT FROZE OVER!

When an experimental serum for hypothermia goes horribly wrong, a small research station in the middle of Antarctica becomes overrun with an army of the frozen dead.

Now a small group of survivors must battle the arctic weather and a horde of frozen zombies as they make their way across the frozen plains of Antarctica to a neighboring research station.

What they don't realize is that they are being hunted by an entity whose sole reason for existing is vengeance; and it will find them wherever they run.

VISIONS OF THE DEAD
A ZOMBIE STORY
by Anthony & Joseph Giangregorio

Jake Roberts felt like he was the luckiest man alive.

He had a great family, a beautiful girlfriend, who was soon to be his wife, and a job, that might not have been the best, but it paid the bills.

At least until the dead began to walk.

Now Jake is fighting to survive in a dead world while searching for his lost love, Melissa, knowing she's out there somewhere.

But the past isn't dead, and as he struggles for an uncertain future, the past threatens to consume him. With the present a constant battle between the living and the dead, Jake finds himself slipping in and out of the past, the visions of how it all happened haunting him. But Jake knows Melissa is out there somewhere and he'll find her or die trying.

In a world of the living dead, you can never escape your past.

INSIDE THE PERIMETER: SCAVENGERS OF THE DEAD
by Alan Spencer

In the middle of nowhere, the vestiges of an abandoned town are surrounded by inescapably high concrete barriers, permitting no trespass or escape. The town is dormant of human life, but rampant with the living dead, who choose not to eat flesh, but to instead continue their survival by cruder means.

Boyd Broman, a detective arrested and falsely imprisoned, has been transferred into the secret town. He is given an ultimatum: recapture Hayden Grubaugh, the cannibal serial killer, who has been banished to the town, in exchange for his freedom.

During Boyd's search, he discovers why the psychotic cannibal must really be captured and the sinister secrets the dead town holds.

With no chance of escape, Broman finds himself trapped among the ravenous, violent dead.

With the cannibal feeding on the animated cadavers and the undead searching for Boyd, he must fulfill his end of the deal before the rotting corpses turn him into an unwilling organ donor.

But Boyd wasn't told that no one gets out alive, that the town is a death sentence. For there is no escape from *Inside the Perimeter*.

DEADFALL
by Anthony Giangregorio

It's Halloween in the small suburban town of Wakefield, Mass.

While parents take their children trick or treating and others throw costume parties, a swarm of meteorites enter the earth's atmosphere and crash to earth.

Inside are small parasitic worms, no larger than maggots.

The worms quickly infect the corpses at a local cemetery and so begins the rise of the undead.

The walking dead soon get the upper hand, with no one believing the truth. That the dead now walk.

Will a small group of survivors live through the zombie apocalypse?

Or will they, too, succumb to the Deadfall.

LOVE IS DEAD: A ZOMBIE ANTHOLOGY
Edited by Anthony Giangregorio
THE DEATH OF LOVE

Valentine's Day is a day when young love is fulfilled.

Where hopeful young men bring candy and flowers to their sweethearts, in hopes of a kiss...or perhaps more. But not in this anthology.

For you see, LOVE IS DEAD, and in this tome, the dead walk, wanting to feed on those same hearts that once pumped in chests, bursting with love.

So toss aside that heart-shaped box of candy and throw away those red roses, you won't need them any longer. Instead, strap on a handgun, or pick up a shotgun and defend yourself from the ravenous undead.
Because in a world where the dead walk, even love isn't safe.

CHILDREN of the VOID
WRITTEN BY:
Anthony Giangregorio
ILLUSTRATED BY:
Andrew Dawe-Collins